The PRAYER of JABEZ™

Devotions for Kids

By Dr. Bruce Wilkinson
Adapted by Rob Suggs
Illustrated by Dan Brawner

Tommy NELSON®
www.tommynelson.com
A Division of Thomas Nelson, Inc.
www.ThomasNelson.com

THE PRAYER OF JABEZ™: DEVOTIONS FOR KIDS

published in Nashville, Tennessee, by Tommy Nelson®,
a division of Thomas Nelson, Inc.

Library of Congress Cataloging-in-Publication Data
Suggs, Rob.
    The prayer of Jabez : devotions for kids living big for God / Bruce Wilkinson ; adapted
by Rob Suggs.
        p. cm.
    Summary: Provides a month's daily readings and reflections that focus on different
aspects of the prayer of Jabez and intended to help explore God's presence in our lives.
    ISBN 0-8499-7945-5
    1. Bible. O.T. Chronicles, 1st, IV, 10—Prayers—History and criticism—Juvenile
literature. 2. Bible. O.T. Chronicles, 1st, IV, 10—Meditations—Juvenile literature. 3.
Christian children—Prayer-books and devotions—English. 4. Jabez (Biblical
figure)—Juvenile literature. [I. Bible. O.T. Chronicles, 1st, IV, 10—Meditations. 2.
Prayer books and devotions.] I. Wilkinson, Bruce. II. Title.

BS1345.6.P68 S83 2001
242'.62—dc21

                                                    2001044564

Design: Koechel Peterson & Associates

Printed in the United States of America
01 02 03 04 05 PHX 9 8 7 6 5 4 3 2 1

Contents

INVITATION

Ready to See Your Life Change?

IF JABEZ WERE AROUND TODAY, I think he would be in shock. After all, people all over the world have discovered his prayer. And since you're reading this book, you're probably one of them!

Upon recovery, I think Jabez would smile and remind you that there's nothing magic about his little prayer. But God's exciting plan for your life is certainly supernatural. It doesn't matter where you are or what your life is like. It's just a prayer away.

Imagine yourself coming face-to-face with God and crying out to Him with your hands and heart open. Then see yourself waiting patiently, courageously, for Him to answer you. That's where the miracles begin. That's when your life will begin to change.

This little book, based on the simple but powerful prayer a common man prayed way back in Bible times, can help you take those steps. It will guide you through a month of daily readings. Each day focuses on a different aspect of the prayer.

Read each devotion, then carefully consider the "Talk Back" questions and statements. I've left space for you to write down some of the new, mind-boggling thoughts that will come to you. Recording these ideas will help you work things out on your own. You can chart your progress, vent your frustrations, and chat with God. As you work your way through this book, you and I will compare adventure stories. And we'll praise God together. In the meantime, may He guide you through this brand-new world. And may He "bless you indeed"!

And Jabez called on the God of Israel saying, "Oh, that You would bless me indeed, and enlarge my territory, that Your hand would be with me, and that You would keep me from evil, that I may not cause pain!"
So God granted him what he requested.
(1 Chronicles 4:10 NKJV)

DAY 1
A SNAPSHOT OF GOD

No one has ever seen this.
No one has ever heard about it. No one has ever imagined
what God has prepared for those who love him.

1 CORINTHIANS 2:9 ICB

THE DREADED DAY has arrived. Today in math class, you'll take up that new thing.

It involves numbers, letters, and strange new concepts. You can remember when your big brother struggled with it, and you've dreaded it ever since. Well, today's the day. Math can be hard enough, but now you've come to the chapter on the new subject: algebra. So, you lean forward in your chair, straining to understand your teacher. No daydreaming today. No doodling in your notebook. This stuff looks big-time hard!

The teacher stands at the blackboard, churning out weird symbols and numbers that don't belong together—at least not as far as you can tell. You copy it all down, of course, but it's as if you're taking up some new language, maybe something spoken on Mars.

Finally, the bell rings. Lunchtime. The other students rush into the hall and head toward the cafeteria where they'll fight for places in line. But you remain planted at your desk. The teacher's face is a question mark as he looks at you. He calls your name and asks, "Do you have a question?"

"Um . . . no sir. I have about *three hundred* questions."

Then he laughs—not a fake, polite laugh, but a deep, throaty one. He comes and sits down at the desk next to yours. This is amazing: Your teacher seems honestly pleased to stay after class and help one student! He's in no hurry at all. You figured the teachers all sprinted to the faculty lounge at lunchtime just like the kids all run for the cafeteria. But your teacher settles in beside you and starts from the beginning, taking it step by step. He seems to know just where the rough places are, and he walks you through them. Ten minutes later, it all comes together. *Yesssss!* You've nailed it—with some great extra help, of course.

GOT THE PICTURE?

Our friend Jabez may have felt just like you at one time. He never would have considered going to God for extra help if he hadn't believed something very important about God. Jabez believed God has time for us and wants to walk us through the rough places in life. And Jabez believed God wants to give us special blessings.

Is that the way you picture God, as a loving Father who wants to help you? Maybe you've swapped school photos with your friends;

after a couple of years, the pictures begin to look out of date. Your friends don't have those strange haircuts anymore, or they've gotten their braces off and their smiles are completely different. In the same way, you could also be carrying (in your mind) a picture of God that needs updating—not because *He* changes, but because *we* find out more about Him. We discover just how much He loves us and wants to help us.

I heard about a guy whose little brother was coloring. The big brother asked, "What are you doing?" The little boy said he was coloring a picture of God. The older brother laughed and said, "But no one knows what God looks like."

Without looking up, the little brother replied, "They will when I'm finished."

THE REAL DEAL

Moses wanted to know what God looks like, so he approached God to get a better picture of Him. Here's the self-portrait God painted for Moses (and for us): "The LORD, the LORD God, merciful and gracious, longsuffering, and abounding in goodness and truth" (Exodus 34:6 NKJV). Now, Moses happened to be one of God's best friends in the Old Testament. He spent days with the Lord, discovering more about Him. And God wanted Moses (and us) to have this big picture: He has mercy on us and blessings for us. He's patient, forgiving, and filled with goodness and truth.

Does that match your picture? Or do you think of Him as a kind of cafeteria monitor of the world, judging your every move—someone who's impatient, unmerciful, and eager to dish out detentions? I've known people who see God that way. Sadly, they miss the wonderful blessings He wants to pour out upon them. I hope you're not one of those people. If you are, throw away that old picture. Replace it with the picture that God gave of Himself to Moses. Isn't that a relief?

Talk to God today just as you'd talk to your very best friend. Ask Him for help just as you'd ask the friendliest teacher you've ever had. He is all that and more. He's the ultimate Father—generous, understanding, and dependable. He knows what you care about. And do you know what *He* cares about? Spending more time with you and blessing you with every good thing.

Why not tell Him how you feel about that?

Day One

TALK BACK

When I hear someone mention God, the first thing I think of is:

Here's what I haven't realized about God until today:

WHAT'S THE BIG IDEA?

If God carries a wallet, it has your snapshot in it—
and He smiles when He looks at it.

DAY 2
LIVING THE BACKSTAGE LIFE

*The Spirit himself testifies with our spirit
that we are God's children. Now if we are children,
then we are heirs—heirs of God and co-heirs with Christ.*
ROMANS 8:16–17 NIV

EVER HEARD THIS ONE? "It's a beautiful day outside. You should be taking advantage of it." Or how about this: "If I were you, I'd take advantage of that wonderful educational software we bought for you."

What's up with adults and this "taking advantage" thing? I guess they feel strongly about getting the best use out of everything—which reminds me of my friend Eric's story. Get ready to groan when you hear the ending.

Eric's favorite group was coming to town for a concert, but there was no way he could afford a ticket. He'd have had to mow practically every lawn in the neighborhood to earn enough. Just when he thought he'd have to hear about it secondhand at school, an incredible thing happened. Eric was the tenth caller on a radio promotion, and he won two tickets to the concert. He could take his number one bud, Angelo, who was always taking Eric places. And since these were the radio station's tickets, they were guaranteed to be pretty good seats. The two friends would see the show without needing binoculars.

Well, the concert night came, and Eric and Angelo had a great time. The music sounded great, and the crowd clearly enjoyed it. The concert featured amazing sets, a laser light show, and smoke that oozed over the stage and onto the floor. The band played three encores. On the way out, Eric decided to stop and buy a T-shirt. When he reached for his wallet, the vendor saw Eric's ticket stub.

"Cool," he said. "So what's the band like in person? What did you guys talk about with them?"

Eric looked at him, puzzled. "What do you mean?" he asked.

"Your ticket, see? It says 'meet and greet' right here. That lets you meet the band backstage before the concert. Most people get autographs, have their picture taken with the band, that sort of thing. Didn't you guys go? I can't believe you missed out on that!"

It was true, of course. In his rush of excitement over getting the tickets, Eric had totally missed the pre-show activities backstage. He and Angelo could have met and talked to members of the band! They could have taken photographs of themselves with the band to show off to their friends. But they hadn't taken advantage of the opportunity that was there for them.

BEHIND THE SMOKE AND LIGHTS

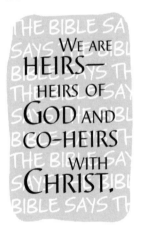

WE ARE HEIRS—HEIRS OF GOD AND CO-HEIRS WITH CHRIST.

I hope those two don't make the same mistake with God. Too many people do. Yesterday you and I discussed how much and how deeply God wants to bless you—up close and personal, you might say. Most Christians are happy just to go to church and sit through the service. But when they do that, they've missed the best part of the whole ticket! God has invited them "backstage" to meet Him personally. Every single Christian has that right, and you're no exception. Why settle for being part of the crowd when you can have a special relationship with your Creator?

Ask yourself this: *Has my faith mostly been about watching a "big show," about sitting with the crowd, or have I gone quietly in prayer to God Himself to experience the awesome things that happen there?*

BEHIND THE

Look at the verse at the beginning of today's reading. If you know Christ as your savior, you're God's child, and sure, that's good news. That gets you in the door. But God has given you greater rights than that because you're His heir. This means He specifically selected you to receive what is His. It's like one of those old movies where the ragged little orphan discovers he is the heir to a major fortune. He gets rid of the rags and begins living in a mansion with butlers, chauffeurs, and a mile-long dinner table. Ever seen that movie?

Well, it's more than a movie. It's the story of your life!

FROM RAGS TO RICHES

On the spiritual side of things, God considers you His heir. And God owns everything in heaven and on Earth. What does that mean for your life? Not necessarily chauffeurs and long dining tables but things that mean much more than material goods. Things that will bring you happiness. Blessings that will make your life count for something big. You have the opportunity to go "backstage" with God and discover what He is really like.

It's as if you've entered a contest and won first prize: a free pass to hang out with the King! When we think of that, who cares about chauffeurs and banquet tables? As a matter of fact, the Bible says, "The Lord's blessing is our greatest wealth" (Proverbs 10:22 TLB).

In Christ, we have all the wealth we need plus the chance to go backstage whenever we feel like it. Now, that's the ticket!

From RAGS TO RICHES

Day Two

TALK BACK

Sometimes I've been a face-in-the-crowd Christian. Here are a few ways I've been God's child without taking that step to fully enjoy being His heir:

Here's what I think my life might be like if I went "backstage" with God:

Today I can take this one specific action to better use my "backstage pass" with God:

WHAT'S THE BIG IDEA?

God is awesome, even when we stay in the crowd, and we have the chance to see Him up close.

DAY 3
ASK GOD

Ask and it will be given to you; seek and you will find; knock and the door will be opened to you. For everyone who asks receives . . .

MATTHEW 7:7–8 NIV

HAVE YOU EVER NOTICED how a word can mean more than you thought? The word *bless* is like that. When you were little, a "blessing" was something you said quickly before dinner. But as you've learned more about Jabez, you've discovered that *blessing* means to give favor and pleasure. A blessing is all that and more! And here's Jabez, a man who went right up to God and asked God to bless him.

The key word here is *asked*. Have you ever really, really wanted something but felt afraid to ask your parents for it? It took courage to ask, but finally you thought, *The worst that can happen is they could say no!* On the other hand, if you didn't ask, you'd get . . . nothing.

Know this about God: He wants to bless you. It brings Him pleasure. But He also wants you to *ask*. It all begins with asking. I spend most of my time traveling and talking to people. I always throw this question at them: "Did you ask God to bless you today?" And you know what I find? Only one person out of one hundred gives me a grin and says yes. The rest look surprised. They don't know they should ask God to bless them. They think it's selfish or believe they already have their share of blessings—as if their share came as a kind of "new member's package deal" when they became Christians! When you receive God's Spirit, you become His heir, as we saw yesterday. But that's a permanent blessing you'll enjoy forever. They're "no-brainers." The Bible says, "God has given us every spiritual blessing in heaven" (Ephesians 1:3 ICB).

GOD'S GIFTS

Imagine it's Christmas morning, and you enter the living room with your family. Your eyes almost pop out of their sockets. Every corner of the room is filled with presents! Hundreds of them in every size and shape. The pile of packages reaches so high you can't even see the Christmas tree, and you can't find a place to sit.

Your family stands there silently. Then someone says, "What should we do?" You all look at each other. No one wants to say what everyone's thinking (*Open the presents! Open the presents!*) because, well, it seems greedy. So, as hard as it may be to imagine, you all ignore those presents. January comes, then June. Years pass, and nobody has opened a single gift. Your family has even had to build new rooms onto the house because those unopened packages have multiplied, and they've taken up all the living space!

ASK AND IT WILL BE GIVEN TO YOU.

I hope you're laughing by now. No, I've never known a family who did this—at least not with real presents. But we all do it with our spiritual blessings, which are much better than any Christmas presents. If I were you, I'd say, "May I please open the gifts? I'd like to start with the purple polka-dotted one shaped like a giant nose!"

Selfish? Not a chance. You're asking for the things God has already reserved for you. He has chosen these gifts as blessings for your benefit. They have to do with your heart's desire and with healing the hurts that bother you. God gives you these gifts to make you a better, happier, stronger person. He wants to do so much for you, but He won't force His blessings on you. He wants you to ask. So, go ahead. Do it right now. Ask God to bless you. Ask Him to give you the blessings He is just waiting to shower upon your life.

TALK BACK

Some things in life are mine simply because I asked someone for them. Here are some examples:

_____

_____

_____

I guess I haven't asked God very often to bless me because:

_____

_____

_____

I'm going to ask God to bless me however He wants, because I know He's just waiting for me to ask! I'll start by saying:

_____

_____

_____

WHAT'S THE BIG IDEA?

*God has packages in heaven
with your name on them—unclaimed.
What's in the first box?
Only one way to find out!*

DAY 4
NOBODIES RULE!

Brothers, look at what you were when God called you.
Not many of you were wise in the way the world judges wisdom.
Not many of you had great influence. Not many of you came
from important families. But God chose the foolish things
of the world to shame the wise. He chose the weak
things of the world to shame the strong. And he chose
what the world thinks is not important.
He chose what the world hates and thinks is nothing.
He chose these to destroy what the world thinks is important.

1 CORINTHIANS 1:26–28 ICB

IF YOU PAY MUCH ATTENTION to Jesus, you'll catch on to one thing right off. He didn't spend much time with the popular crowd. He insisted on hanging out with people the "in" crowd usually ignored. Jesus chose characters that we might call losers or loners today. He really loved the weak, the outcasts, and the ones who came from poor families. He healed them. He hung out with them and traveled with them. (You can look it up!) And He asked twelve of them to be His disciples.

But it wasn't just Jesus. The idea of "nobodies" being important in God's eyes stretches all the way through the Bible. Jabez wasn't a part of the Bible's popular crowd. Read 1 Chronicles, and you'll find that he came from a group of no-names such as Ezer, Koz, and Anub. We have no clue what Jabez actually did with his life, but we know God honored him. This fellow should have been totally forgotten by now, but here you are, thousands of years later, reading a book about him!

The truth is that God loves nobodies.

YOU GO, AGNES!

Here's a name that's just about as exciting as Anub: Agnes Bojaxhiu. Ever heard of her? Well, she was just another "nobody" who never attended college, never got married, never owned a car. Like Jesus, she hung out with the lowest of the low. And among those poor, hungry people, God used her. One by one, Agnes cared for thousands of starving, poor, sick people. When friends asked her about it, Agnes would only say she wanted "to belong to Jesus." By the time she died, she'd shown thousands of others how to take care of poor and sick people, too. But none of those others called her Agnes. They and the world knew her as Mother Teresa. You can probably find a book or two about her in your school library. Today the ministry she began cares for half a million hungry families every year.

While Mother Teresa was still alive, someone asked her, "What will happen when you're no longer with us?"

She replied, "I believe that if God finds a person even more useless than me, He will do even greater things through her."

She got the message: God loves to use "useless" people.

UN-COOL IS COOL

"What, *me* ask for God's blessing?" I hear you say with a little doubt in your voice. "I guess He'd bless me if I really earned it, but I'm always messing up. Just ask anybody."

If I asked you to name all the things you don't like about yourself, you probably could give me a long list. Well, welcome to the club. We all have lists like yours. We all have weak spots. And we've all gone to bed wondering, *Will I ever get things right?*

The answer to that question is no. You'll never be perfect, and neither will any of your friends. But that's not the point. The important thing is that God has big plans for you, anyway! If your life feels like a mess sometimes, you're Jesus' kind of person. He would love to hang out with you, because He knows you won't pretend to be some superhero who doesn't have problems. You're just the kind of person He'd like to have as a disciple. If you're un-cool . . . that's cool! You're like Mother Teresa. And like Jabez.

A CHECKUP FROM THE NECK UP

Let's get inside your head for a moment. You probably think that in the game of life, you're a bench-sitter, a fifth-string right fielder. You figure that only the real superstars (do you know a few of those?) can play this blessing-asking game. You think Jesus won't want to use someone with a messy room and who argues too much and isn't the smartest kid at school.

Knowing your weak points is the first step toward doing something great for God. Jabez asked God to keep him from causing any pain. But he also asked God to bless him and to do great things through him. A lot of amazing people in this world have started in

your place. But instead of focusing on what they couldn't do, they focused on what they *could* do—with God's blessing.

God knew you even before you were born. He formed you in your mother's body (it says so right there in Psalm 139:13). He knew all about you even before He placed you here on Earth. And He knows the incredible adventures He wants you to have. He's not waiting for you to find the secret of living without mistakes (there isn't one). At this very moment

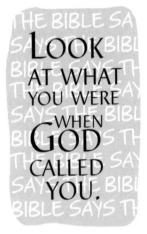

LOOK AT WHAT YOU WERE WHEN GOD CALLED YOU.

He's waiting for you to come to Him with open hands and say, "Lord, I am weak but You are strong. I'm not exactly perfect, but You are. I need Your blessing! Please, Lord, bless me a lot. Bless me today!"

Day Four

TALK BACK

Sure, I've been mad at myself because of the things I do wrong. Take this example:

But based on what we've talked about today, here's how God responds to me even though I'm less than perfect:

That should make a difference in how I think about God and how I talk to Him. Here's what I'm going to do from now on:

WHAT'S THE BIG IDEA?

In the eyes of Jesus, there's no such thing as a loser. Everybody who asks for His blessings wins big!

Day 5
The Game of the Name

Then you will have a new name.
The Lord himself will give you that new name.
Isaiah 62:2 ICB

"What should we name the baby?"

Ever heard a family trying to figure that one? Nobody seems to agree on that perfect name. But most of us would agree Jabez got stuck with an awful name. Jabez's mom insisted on giving her baby a name that, in Hebrew, means "pain."

Listen, I'm not going to say anything bad about Jabez's mother. She certainly raised a godly young man. But I can't help wondering why she called her child the Hebrew equivalent of "Ouch!"

Do you think I'm joking? Read 1 Chronicles 4:9, and you'll see that Jabez got stuck with a rather embarrassing moniker (a fancy word for "name"). Worse still, ancient people believed a name could predict a person's future. They believed a girl named Lovely, for example, would grow in beauty and a boy named Clever would become a good businessman. On the other hand, anyone named Jabez was bound to be a pain! It was quite a lot for a little guy to overcome as he grew into his place in the world.

But you know what? It's not where you start that counts. It's not how many brick walls block your path. The only thing that matters is where you finish. Actually, sometimes it *helps* to have a setback of some kind. I'll give you a good example. Her name is Joni Eareckson Tada. I don't know what her name means, but it ought to mean "overcomer." You see, Joni suffered a terrible diving accident when she was a young athlete. She was confined to a wheelchair, unable to walk or use her hands. So, what did she do?

Well, she quickly became an outstanding artist, using only her teeth to guide the pen or brush. Her paintings and drawings are treasured everywhere. She has written nearly thirty books, and many of them have won awards. She's even become a recording star with her own tapes and CDs. But what impresses me most is that she started a wonderful ministry to help thousands of disabled people and cheer them on toward success.

THE LORD HIMSELF WILL GIVE YOU THAT NEW NAME.

Pretty good for someone without the use of hands and legs, wouldn't you agree? Her "disability" just made her more determined to develop *other* abilities.

And God has blessed her indeed.

CHECK YOUR NAMETAG

Here's an idea you might enjoy. Jabez had a name that means pain; what name would you give yourself? How would you describe your life in one simple name? How about Awesome Athlete or Super Scholar or Web-ster?

You can have fun with this. But you should also realize that many of us give ourselves invisible nametags without even realizing it—nametags that say Bad Grades, Unattractive, or Unathletic. We gather those ideas after disappointments, and after a while, they become little invisible labels that can cling to us for years. These labels can be hard to pry off. And they can affect our lives because they're always there to remind us: *I can't do this! I failed in the past, so I'm bound to fail again.* Those long-ago people were right after all: Names *can* make a difference. I'm glad Jabez ignored his label.

Let this idea stick to you: God has His own set of labels, and He covers us with them. Would you like to hear a few?

1. "Chosen" (John 15:19 ICB)
2. "Mine" (Psalm 50:10–12 ICB)
3. "Beloved" (Deuteronomy 33:12 NKJV)
4. "Sought After" (Isaiah 62:12 NIV)

And here's one that sums it all up: "Friend" (James 2:23 ICB).

THE NAME THAT STICKS

Once upon a time, there was a man who loved to fish. His name was Simon, and he set aside his nets to follow Jesus. Simon was a fireball; he always acted without thinking and often blurted out exactly the wrong thing at the wrong time. But Jesus liked Simon anyway. He had a special place in His heart for this bumbling apostle. One day He looked at him and said, "You are blessed, Simon. . . . I tell you, you are *Peter*" (Matthew 16:17–18 ICB, emphasis mine). In other words, Jesus blessed Simon by giving him a new name. He stuck a label on him that means "Rock."

Peter hadn't acted much like a rock in the past (except for occasionally behaving like he had rocks in his head), but in time, he became firm and strong, like a ten-ton boulder. He had been cowardly, but soon he became courageous. He had been confused, but soon he clearly understood what was true and what was false. His faith was rock-solid. The name that Jesus gave him stuck.

Jesus gives *you* a name, too, and it's the only name that matters. Let me assure you, the name He has for you is beautiful and powerful. It's a name that says He wants to bless you in the same way He blessed Simon Peter.

Pull off those other tags—*rrrriiip!*—and Jesus' name for you will stick to you forever.

TALK BACK

A week ago I might have made these nametags for myself:

_____

_____

_____

_____

But here are the names I now know God has given me:

_____

_____

_____

_____

_____

If I carry these names with me at all times, here is how my life might change:

_____

_____

_____

_____

WHAT'S THE BIG IDEA?

Sticks and stones may break my bones,
but God's names for me will always heal me.

Week One

DAY 6
GOD'S BEST FOR YOU

*Trust in the LORD and do good; dwell in the land
and enjoy safe pasture. Delight yourself in the LORD
and he will give you the desires of your heart.*

PSALM 37:3–4 NIV

DO YOU KEEP notebooks in school? Maybe you have binders for different subjects: language, math, social studies, and science. They help you organize assignments, notes, tests, and all kinds of things.

I'm not in school anymore, but I still keep a notebook. Mine covers several subjects: family, church, friends, work, and fun. These are things I pray about, and my notebook helps me keep track of my prayer requests. I found out a long time ago that if I didn't keep a written record of my prayers, I'd forget all about them. If I didn't keep track, God would answer prayers I'd forgotten about praying. Then I'd miss a lot of the wonderful answers He sends me.

I write down all my prayer requests, then I tell them to God, one by one. Every day, before God and I get together, I go over that book. I write the answers I've received, "yes" or "no" or "maybe later," next to the things I'm praying about. (As you might guess, my favorites are the ones with "yes" next to them!)

IT CAN'T HURT TO ASK
One day as I was enjoying a Bible study with some of my friends, I decided to let them see my prayer notebook. I showed them all the sections. They could see what kinds of things I'd asked for and how God had answered. My friends were amazed to see the hundreds of

prayer requests I'd made, each one with an account of God's response (yes, no, or maybe later).

HE WILL GIVE YOU THE DESIRES OF YOUR HEART,

But one of my friends became very upset. "Are you trying to tell me we should pray for things we *want*?" he bellowed.

"Why would God want you to pray for what you *don't* want?" I replied. "If you want a fancy car and you ask for it, God will answer you. He might say yes, or He might say no. If it's something that isn't good for you, He'll say no. Or He'll give you what you asked for, just to teach you a lesson you need to learn. (One important lesson is that some of the things we expect to make us happy often do just the opposite.) Either way, He'll be delighted that you trusted Him enough to ask."

Wow! Does that mean you can ask God for things other than world peace or a blessing on the food? Can you ask Him for stuff that you really want, like a mountain bike or a new CD player? Sure. It's all about being yourself when you and God are together. He knows what's inside you, so there's no reason to hide what you want and what you're thinking. Think about our talk a few days ago. We need to remember that snapshot of God that shows He loves to please us. But He also loves to give us what we really *need*—and what we'd want if we were smart enough to ask for it! That's the key to this portion of Jabez's prayer: trusting God to give us what *He* determines is best for us.

When you ask for blessings with trust in your heart, God happily answers. As you see the ways God blesses you, your faith will grow stronger and stronger. You'll want even more of what He wants—and nothing else. It's the whole secret of life, but you have my permission to share this secret with as many people as you'd like.

Day Six

Talk Back

I've been afraid to pray about some things because:

_____

_____

_____

_____

Today I learned one "big idea" about talking to God. Here it is, in my own words:

_____

_____

_____

Today I'm going to trust God to give me what I really need. I'll use this space to say a few words to Him:

_____

_____

_____

What's the Big Idea?

Tell Him what you want,
and ask Him to give you what you need.
Then, increasingly, they'll become the same thing.

DAY 7
WHAT LIMITS?

"Test me in this," says the LORD *Almighty,*
"and see if I will not throw open the floodgates of heaven
and pour out so much blessing
that you will not have room enough for it."
MALACHI 3:10 NIV

YOUR FIRST DAY in a new school—that's a tough one, isn't it? Do you remember walking into an entire building full of strangers? There you stood, surrounded by the loud crowd in the hallway, and yet you probably felt so alone.

The new teachers seemed scary enough, but the cafeteria woman—well, she looked like something out of a late-night horror movie! She stared at you so sternly that you didn't even want to look back.

But then something happened that caught you by surprise. It turned out that the cafeteria monitor, once you got to know her, wasn't so bad at all. Now she smiles and even laughs with you sometimes! She remembers your name, and she's eager to help you. Wow, did you have her pegged wrong!

As we've seen before, many of us make that same mistake about God. We think He's watching us from heaven like the referee in a soccer match. We believe He's making sure we don't break any rules, and if we do, He blows His whistle and sends some trouble thundering through our lives. But what kind of God do you find when you get close to Him? He's a God who says, "Look out below! I'm pouring out the blessings, and I don't want you to drown!"

YOU'LL NEVER GET TO THE BOTTOM OF THIS!

Actually, the "quote" I just gave you is my translation of Malachi 3:10, our verse for today. Read it again. Have you ever seen floodgates? Have you ever seen a film showing floodwaters breaking through a dam? There's unbelievable power in water that's been held back and suddenly breaks loose. Entire towns have been washed away when dams have burst.

God gives us such a word picture in the Bible for a reason. The good things He has stored up for us have piled up behind the gates of heaven. He wants to let them flow out, releasing incredible power into our lives and the world. He simply wants us to say the word, so He can send those blessings splashing over us. But there's one fact that's hard to wrap our minds around: God's blessings are *infinite*. That means His reservoir will never run dry. The floodgates will never see the last of the blessings surging out toward you and me. It means we can't get to the bottom of God's goodness. It goes on and on and on.

I once heard a story about a 350-pound football player who walked into a pizza place where a sign promised, "All the Pepperoni Pizza You Can Eat!" He polished off twelve pizzas before the manager came to his table and said, "Okay, that's all you can eat! We're out of pepperoni!"

Unlike the sign in that pizza shop's window, the one in heaven's window is trustworthy. It promises, "All the blessings you can handle." And believe me: It's all you can handle!

THE CASE OF THE BOTTOMLESS BASKET

Do you believe you can have more than your share of blessings? Some people think so, but it's not true. There's no limit to the blessings of God. You'll never hear Him say, "I'm sorry, but there's been a run on blessings today, and I'm completely out of stock. Jason, the kid across the street from you, has been hoarding blessings, and he got your share."

We know better than that, don't we? God can bless you and bless you and bless you some more, and it won't take away from anyone else's blessings. He really does want to give you all the good things He has planned for you. Do you remember the story of Jesus and the loaves and fish? Check it out in Mark 8. There was a big, hungry crowd and not a restaurant in sight—just a few small fish and a couple of loaves of bread. Jesus blessed the food, then the disciples walked through

SO MUCH **BLESSING** THAT YOU WILL **NOT** HAVE **ROOM** ENOUGH FOR IT.

the crowd, carrying it in a basket. And every time they reached into the basket, there was just as much food as there had been before.

It was an "All You Can Eat" deal, for real! The Bible tells us that when no one could take another bite, there were still seven large baskets of food left. I can just see the frustration in all those "clean your plate" moms who were present! The plate God serves you can never be emptied, because He always has more. The moms of the world will just have to deal with it!

ALL THE EXTRAS

There's one other thing I hope you'll see about God and His blessings. He gives us things beyond our wildest dreams. I don't know what kinds of good things God heaps on you. He knows, better than I do, what delights you best. The main thing is that you realize just how kind He really is. The more you know Him, the better it gets. You'll never reach the bottom of that basket.

Day Seven

TALK BACK

When I was younger, I thought some funny things about God. Here are some of them:

_____

_____

_____

Now I can see how much He loves to bless me. I'm going to stop and list some of the blessings He's given me lately:

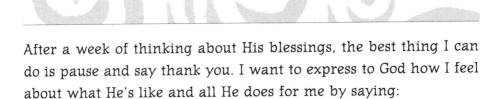

After a week of thinking about His blessings, the best thing I can do is pause and say thank you. I want to express to God how I feel about what He's like and all He does for me by saying:

WHAT'S THE BIG IDEA?

When you stand in the shower of God's blessings,
it makes you want to sing!

Day 8
Ready for Action

Ask whatever you wish, and it will be given you.
This is to my Father's glory, that you bear much fruit,
showing yourselves to be my disciples.

John 15:7–8 niv

Imagine the finger of God, hovering over the "directory" of heaven. That finger starts at the A section and moves downward, line after line, column after column. God is looking for a certain name. He wants to find the one that stands out from the rest. And where does His finger hesitate, then stop?

Look closely. It has stopped at *your* name!

And why has He chosen you? Because you're moving into your second week of the Jabez journey. You're telling Him that you want *more* out of life—more blessings, more excitement, more usefulness—and you want what He wants for you. God respects that.

And that brings us to what we might call Jabez Phase 2—the pioneer prayer. You've probably studied pioneers in school. They left their well-known surroundings. They moved in horse-drawn wagons to the wide-open spaces of the West. On the rolling prairie and the great, flat plains, they built cabins out of sod or whatever they could find. They staked out new land and began new lives.

The pioneers faced surprises and dangers at every turn. But they thrived on adventure and challenge, and they loved finding out what waited for them around the next bend in the road. The Jabez journey is a pioneer's adventure, especially here in Phase 2. Jabez prayed, ". . . enlarge my territory." Some Bible versions use the word *borders* instead of *territory*; others say, "Give me more land." Jabez wanted to move out and establish new, wider borders, just as the pioneers did. But for you and me today, the request means, "Give me more responsibility, Lord, more opportunity. Help me make a greater impact on my friends and my world."

Are you ready to take the challenge?

MOVING THE MARKERS

Why should we expand those borders, anyway? Jabez probably worked with land and livestock for a living. The more land and animals he owned, the more important he became. Jabez wanted to do something big for God, and he knew he needed more land to make it happen.

ASK WHATEVER YOU WISH, AND IT WILL BE GIVEN YOU,

What about you—more land? Most likely, all you've got is your bedroom, and you couldn't even fit a single cow in there! So how does this part of the prayer apply to you?

Think about it. Jabez was asking for much more than land. He was also asking for more chances to serve God. You should ask God for the same thing: more chances to show other people what it means to live God's way. Ask God to help you go more places and do better things. And ask Him for opportunities to do better things where you already are. There are a million different possibilities.

You don't need to decide right now how you'll increase your territory. One great thing about the Jabez adventure is that you leave the details up to God. You trust Him to bless you His way, and you trust Him to expand your borders where He wants them expanded. And you know you're going to grow through whatever He decides. That makes things simpler, doesn't it?

BORDER PATROL

Here's the challenge. Ask God to enlarge your territory, then watch closely to see what happens in your life. Patrol those borders. Maybe you'll have a chance to help a younger student with a homework assignment. Maybe you'll be able to help an elderly person in your neighborhood by running errands or doing a little yard work. I like to think of these opportunities as "Jabez moments." Who knows when one of them will occur in your life? Half the fun comes from discovering the opportunities that God brings you!

When they happen, I guarantee you they will bring you satisfaction. (Remember, God is blessing you, not giving you extra homework!) He knows what you do best, because He made you. He knows what kinds of things you care about. He wants to give you more and expand your borders in those areas of your life.

God has been waiting for this day a long time. He's excited that you have come to Him and said, "Lord, I'm ready to rumble! Let me do more things for You." He's excited about showing you new opportunities and new adventures for your life. He's thrilled to have you as His partner in projects that will make this world a better place. That's what happens when you ask God to expand your territory. You become His partner.

Your partnership with God will continue all through your life as you pray the prayer again and again. Your borders will expand to a truly awesome size as God continues to answer your prayer. But for now, just a little bit more territory will do. Watch for God to give you something new and exciting.

It's bound to happen. After all, He has circled your name in the directory of heaven.

TALK BACK

I've never thought much about territory or borders before. Now I see they relate to all the things and places where I'm involved, including:

I wouldn't be surprised if God gave me new things to do in these places:

And finally, here's where I pray the first two parts of the Jabez prayer: "Oh, that You would bless me indeed, and enlarge my territory." I'll put those two parts of the prayer in my own words as I ask God to bless me and give me more to do for Him:

WHAT'S THE BIG IDEA?

Every day has a new opportunity for me.
The important thing is to ask God
to help me recognize it.

Day 9
TELL ME ABOUT MY TERRITORY

Open your eyes.
Look at the fields that are ready for harvesting now.
JOHN 4:35 ICB

THE MAIL SEEMS TO BRING me a new surprise every day. I have friends in many places who have started praying the prayer of Jabez. They can't wait to tell me about their miracles and blessings.

Take Amanda from Florida, for example. She can't believe this new thing. As soon as she began to pray the Jabez prayer, God opened up opportunities for her to talk about Jesus to her friends at school. She hadn't done that very often in the past, but now she enjoys sharing all the things she has learned about Jesus.

At the same time, Amanda has found herself in frequent situations where she can help people deal with problems. How amazing to hear about the differences she's making for God in other people's lives! She attends the same school and lives in the same house as before. But now God gives her more chances to be useful, more Jabez moments, because she has asked Him to do so.

Amanda got so excited, she had to start writing down the things that have happened—just like I do in my prayer notebook. She doesn't want to lose track of all the great experiences she's having. So she keeps a record of all her Jabez moments, knowing that when she reads through them later, she'll shake her head and say, "Did that really happen to *me?*"

ONE STEP AT A TIME

Maybe you're not too sure about all this. After all, who knows what sorts of things God might send your way? I know Amanda felt unsure before she decided to ask God to expand her territory. But she trusted that He would never give her more than she could handle. She knew He would bring her opportunities that fit her perfectly.

Please keep in mind that God will always go with you, and He'll always give you the strength you need. God's territory is the whole world, but for right now, maybe the whole neighborhood or just the whole class is enough for you. In time, you can always ask God for more, then more, then more again as you grow older and wiser and stronger. Maybe today you'll pray, "Let me serve You in my school, Lord." Someday you may pray, "Let me serve You in my city, my country, or throughout my world." Those territories can come later.

God knows where your borders are at this particular moment, and He knows how far to move them outward. Some people's borders reach around entire countries. A few even claim the whole world as their territory. I hope that as you grow older you'll read about Christians who have claimed entire cities and nations for God. You'll see how they've helped hundreds of thousands of people get to know Jesus.

FINDING START

For now the question remains, where is *your* territory?

That's something God will have to show you. But one thing is certain right now: You *do* have territory. It might be as small as your family. Maybe you'll expand your borders by being a better brother or sister, or a better son or daughter. You might draw the lines a little wider and include your neighborhood. How can you serve God there? Maybe your borders extend to your school, your church, or the other places we've discussed. As you consider how to begin, picture a board game. There's usually a space marked *Start* where you go to make your first move. That's what to look for in your life as you seek ways to expand your borders for God.

God just helped a ninth grader named Justin find his *Start*. When Justin tried to think of what he did well, all he could come up with was his working on the computer. *No way God can use that*, he thought. But he thought wrong! As soon as he began looking to expand his borders for God, Justin was given a chance to design a Web site for his school. Afterward, the school recognized him with a special link to his own Web page: "Learn more about Justin, our site designer". There, on his own personal home page, he mentions that he follows Jesus. And visitors to Justin's page can "click here" to find out more about Christianity. Talk about territorial expansion!

THE FIRST CLUE

You've got to love how God enlarged Amanda's and Justin's borders. And He did it by simply giving them more of the things they already did well or enjoyed. If you're curious to discover where God will expand your territory, think about the things you get satisfaction from. Think about the little chores and helpful things you can do for others that make you feel good afterward.

And remember: God isn't likely to drop you into the lion's cage at the zoo. He won't ask you to clean up the entire city's garbage or mow every lawn in the county. He loves you a lot and will work with your strengths. He knows what you'll do with excellence.

So, what's it going to be for you?

Day Nine

TALK BACK

Doing more for God can be exciting or frightening. Here's how I honestly feel about doing more for God:

_____

_____

Here are some ways God may help me make a greater impact on my friends and my world for Him:

With family members:

_____

At school:

_____

At church:

_____

In the neighborhood:

_____

WHAT'S THE BIG IDEA?

*Faith is going to the edge of your borders—
and taking one more step.*

Day 10
MAKING THE MOST OF TIME

For we are God's workmanship,
created in Christ Jesus to do good works,
which God prepared in advance for us to do.
EPHESIANS 2:10 NIV

"WHAT'S THAT? Do more for God? How am I going to fit it in?" you ask.

"Get real! I wake up early every morning, gobble down a bowl of cereal, and hurry off to school. Then I'm stuck inside that building for the best hours of my day. It's not like I can raise my hand and say, 'Yo! Miss Thornthistle! I need to cruise across town for a few minutes to expand my borders. Look for me sometime after gym class.'

"After school," you sigh, "there's a jillion hours of homework, for starters. Then I have chores to do, dinner to eat, maybe a few minutes of TV or a computer game. I go to bed, wake up, and start all over again! I'm not even going to mention the sports and other activities I have at different parts of the year. Being more useful to God sounds great, but where am I supposed to find the time?"

Hey, I hear you, and I just want to say . . . relax! As I talk to kids who are making it happen and doing bigger things for God, I don't see any of them checking out of class. I don't see anybody skipping homework or baseball or cheerleading or scouting. Here's one border we can't get past: The day has exactly twenty-four hours. I haven't yet figured out a way to come up with twenty-five. God set those limits, so He must have a way for us to get the job done in the time He has given us. I challenge you to discover how God can use your time better.

SAME HOUR, NEW POWER

Ashley, for example, spends most of her time either in school or on the soccer field. She told God, "Help, Lord, I'm booked up! I can't find any more hours in my day, but I trust You to be creative with what I've got. Please use me better at soccer practice and during class time." Then, with a heavy sigh of relief, she turned back to her busy schedule and trusted God to do His thing.

And did He ever! In almost no time at all, Ashley had a big grin plastered across her face. She said she suddenly realized how much time she spends at soccer sitting on the bench, waiting for her turn on the field. Instead of chatting that time away with Stephanie, her best friend, she's branching out and getting better acquainted with her other teammates. Now she has many close friends on the team, not just two or three. God has expanded her territory without taking her away from soccer. And she's enjoying soccer more than ever.

Ashley said the same thing has happened at school. For one thing, she has tried to make one new friend every week during lunch or in gym class, where she has a chance to move around and get acquainted. And she's made some great new friends.

Ashley's best subject is science, and she found out quickly how God could use that. Now Ashley keeps an eye out for kids who are having a hard time. She's amazed how often she finds a moment or two to answer questions or offer helpful tips. Suddenly Ashley is a big hero among the science strugglers.

And what do you think the teacher is saying about Ashley? I'll give you a hint: It's a good thing!

THREE SIGNS THAT GOD IS USING YOU

I've noticed that God does at least three things when He gets involved with your time:

First, He shows you people who need help with something. He sends excellent opportunities your way on a daily basis. Soon you find yourself thinking, *I see what You're doing, God! You sent this person to me, and I'm supposed to help him or her.*

Second, your schedule won't change, but it will fill up with more opportunities than it used to have. You'll make more friends, serve others better, and become more accomplished than you were before you asked God to help you.

GOD PREPARED IN ADVANCE FOR US!

Third, you'll expand your borders in some areas and reduce them in others. That's what Ashley has done by giving up just a little bit of her time with Stephanie, her best friend. She still has plenty of time with Stephanie, but now Ashley's sharing time with the other girls, too.

God knows you're becoming mature and wise when you make this kind of choice, and He rewards you in special ways. Time isn't a problem when you serve God. After all, He's the One in charge of time. (He's good at science, too!) Ask God to take charge of your day and to bring more miracles to your moments. You'll be amazed at how much quality you can squeeze out of the same quantity of time in your day.

Day Ten

TALK BACK

The things that take up the most time in my daily schedule are:

_____

_____

_____

Opportunities for helping others during my day include:

_____

_____

_____

God can use my time better than I can. Each morning this week I'll hand my day over to Him and trust Him to use me during my regular routine. I'll ask Him right now with these words:

_____

_____

_____

WHAT'S THE BIG IDEA?

You can't find more time by serving God,
but you can put more of God in your time.

Day 11
FEARLESS

Remember that I commanded you to be strong and brave.
So don't be afraid. The Lord your God will be with you everywhere you go.

JOSHUA 1:9 ICB

QUICK! What's your greatest fear?

For some, it's climbing that long rope in PE. For others, it's that little moment at the amusement park just before the big plunge on the Roller Coaster of Doom. For some of us, it's . . . spinach! But here's something that scares all of us: moving into new territory. It could be starting at a new school, moving into a new neighborhood, or joining a new team.

Many of the Bible's greatest heroes knew what it was like to feel afraid. Abraham, Ruth, Moses, Gideon, Esther, David, and many others went somewhere new and did something difficult for God. But before they could, they had to face their own fears.

Just before Jesus went to heaven after His resurrection, He told His disciples, "Don't be afraid." And He gave them this incredible promise: ". . . I will be with you always. I will continue with you until the end of the world" (Matthew 28:10, 20 ICB). When you have to do something or go somewhere scary, remember Jesus' words.

Look at the verse at the beginning of this reading again. God said those words to Joshua when it was time to cross the Jordan River into the Promised Land. A wonderful new home awaited Joshua and his people across that river, but it was filled with scary enemies who were ready to fight. The more powerful enemy, however, was the people's own fear.

Fear can beat you before the enemy ever gets a shot. And your fear is usually linked with mistaken ideas. For example, you may think, *I can't do this. I'm not good enough. The other kids are better than I am. I'm on my own. No one will help me.*

NO FEAR

But here's another way to head into a new challenge. Tell yourself, "I can do this! God has given me talents and gifts. He made this opportunity because He loves me. I can do all things through Christ who gives me strength. Wherever I go, He goes with me!"

Get the idea? We can be fearless because He is right here, 24/7! When you go into a scary situation with this frame of mind, you go in power, and you're much more likely to finish your task. It's like that bumper sticker I've seen on lockers, bikes, skateboards, and notebooks: No Fear. One statement, two words—plain and simple. Walking into a new challenge knowing that God is with you, that's having no fear. Okay, you may feel a little nervous, but remember the main thing: God is bigger than any fear you might feel.

You're in a place in life where you must constantly face new borders, strange territories, and greater challenges. Each grade in school has something new and different about it. Every year you make

THE BIBLE SAYS:
GOD WILL BE WITH YOU EVERYWHERE.

new friends, and sometimes the old ones move away or go to different schools. There's a first time for everything, and it seems you're dealing with a first time in something every day. Isn't it nice to know that God goes with you the first time—and every time? This is a supernatural gift. And God promises this gift whenever you move into a new and frightening place. He goes with you, and He gives you His power. (You'll learn more about that second one next week.)

YOU AND ME, LORD

Michael's family moved to a new city. And if that wasn't tough enough, Michael would be in the youngest class of his new school. All summer he dreaded that first day when he'd have to find his locker and ask where to go all day long and not know anyone. Toward the end of the summer, he thought about it every night as he drifted off to sleep. Would he measure up? Would the other kids accept him? Would the schoolwork be tougher?

Michael wasn't fearless. He was just as nervous as you or I might be. But he tried to concentrate on the fact that God knew just how he felt. And God wouldn't say, "Deal with it, kid! Come on, get tough!" God truly cares. He placed a strong hand on Michael's shoulder. Then He smiled and said, "This is a whole new world, isn't it? How about You and I go together? We'll get through it. You'll see."

No matter what happened, no matter how the other kids acted, no matter how tough the classes got, Michael never felt truly alone. And as the first day turned into the first week and then the first month, he felt increasingly like a champion.

The same thing happened to Joshua when he had a river to cross. It happened to Moses when he had a sea to cross. It happened to Ruth when she had a new land to enter. It happened to David when he had to hide while an entire army hunted for him. On this side of things, there's a lot of fear and uncertainty. But on the other side, there's a victory party! So, put on your No Fear attitude and climb that rope. Ride that roller coaster. Take on that new school . . . or whatever God has laid before you. The party will be great.

You & Me LORD

Day Eleven

TALK BACK

I guess the thing that frightens me most right now is this:

If Jesus were sitting right beside me, here's what I think He would say to me about my worries:

If Jesus were sitting right beside me, here's what I think He would say to me about my worries:

Knowing God is with me, here's how I'm going to face up to my fears:

WHAT'S THE BIG IDEA?

Courage isn't the lack of fears.
It's the willingness to move forward in spite of them.

DAY 12
COMFORT ZONES

Don't lose your courage or be afraid.
Don't panic or be frightened.
The Lord your God goes with you.

DEUTERONOMY 20:3–4 ICB

I GET A BIG KICK out of watching a turtle. Slowly but surely, it plods along until it senses anything remotely threatening. Then— *zip*—the head tucks in, and—*zip*—the legs retract, and—*zip*—the tail disappears. All that's left is one solid, locked-up, heavy-duty shell. The turtle has retreated to its comfort zone.

I think there's a little bit of turtle in each of us. We may not wear shells on our backs, but we do carry comfort zones in our minds. In some situations we feel safe. Others make us want to scurry back into the safety of our little shells. How about this one: being with a group of older kids you don't know too well. It's easy to feel out of your comfort zone then, isn't it? Will they pick on you? Will they make you feel small and insignificant?

Everybody has a comfort zone. I know a lot of adults who are afraid to tell God, "I'll go anywhere You want me to go." When I ask them why, they say something like, "If I tell Him that, He might send me to a jungle!" They can picture themselves stumbling through the steaming equator, fending off the snakes. But here's the funny thing: When I have the same conversation with people who live in the jungle, they tell me, "If I make myself totally available to God, He might send me to a major city with no trees and only tall buildings!"

Different comfort zones for different people.

BRING ON THE MOUNTAIN!

When God leads you out of your comfort zone, you have to be like Caleb, who was one of the greatest soldiers in Israel's history. He and Joshua sneaked into the Promised Land with ten other spies. Remember? The Timid Ten felt the land was out of their comfort zone. The land was occupied by giants, and they were too afraid to even think of moving there. Not Joshua and Caleb! They wanted to grab the land God had prepared for them. But the ten "turtle"-thinkers outvoted them. As a result, Israel wandered for forty years in the

THE BIBLE SAYS

DON'T LOSE YOUR COURAGE OR BE AFRAID.

desert. Get it? They wouldn't leave their comfort zone to go where God had led them, so they got stuck in a place that was *worse.*

Forty-five years later, Joshua and Caleb were still chasing after real estate. They had grown old by then, but Caleb still had his eye on a certain mountain promised to him by God all those years earlier. He was ready to seize that mountain even if he had to fight for it. When Joshua gave the okay, Caleb led the attack.

Here's the point: Wonderful blessings are waiting for you, but turtles need not apply. God wants those who are willing to leave their shells.

AGES, STAGES, AND ZONES

Have you ever noticed how comfort zones get bigger with age? For infants, the zone is their parents' arms; babies often cry when others try to hold them. For two-year-olds, the comfort zone might be behind a parent's legs, peering around to see what's going on. As we mature, our comfort zones keep expanding, and it's a scary adjustment every time.

Can you remember the last time you took a big step into a new zone? How did you feel just before you did it? How did you feel after you succeeded? It's amazing, isn't it? You learn to ride a bicycle, then a skateboard, then Rollerblades, then water skis, then snow skis—then, hey, where's that parachute? I admit, skydiving is beyond my comfort zone! I'm not there yet. But as I've moved out of my zones before, I've noticed this cycle:

- ☯ **Comfort.** I'm relaxed in my current zone, but I have my eyes on a new mountain.
- ☯ **Discomfort.** I'm right on the borderline, and my stomach is tied in knots! I'm tempted to turn back, but God helps me take the mountain.
- ☯ **Comfort.** Yesssss! I made it! I'm pumped, thankful to God, and I relax again. But what's that just over the horizon? A taller mountain . . .

The first year Megan had to sell Girl Scout cookies, her mom did most of the work as they made their way through their neighborhood. Megan and her mom walked to each door together, then Megan rang the bell and showed the order form while her mom did the talking. Megan was a little shy, but she managed.

The next year her mom insisted that Megan do more of the selling herself. Megan said, "Why can't we do it like last year?" But she stretched herself a little further and forced herself to ask each neighbor, "Would you like to buy some Girl Scout cookies?" And each time she asked, it became a little easier. This year she and her mom are setting up a booth outside the grocery store, and Megan will ask complete strangers to buy cookies. That's tough! But she remembers how God helped her be brave before, and she knows He'll help her again.

It's never easy to move on to bigger and better things, but it's never boring, either. And it's always worthwhile. That thrill of taking new ground for God, doing something bigger, is all the reward you need.

Day Twelve

TALK BACK

Here's a map of my comfort zones with a turtle (that's me!) in the middle. My shell is my biggest comfort zone. This could be a feeling—like fear or shyness—or anything that keeps me from doing bigger and better things for God. My biggest comfort zone (or shell!) is _____. Circling me are other layers of comfort zones. I will label each of them. Now I can see exactly what steps I can take to move beyond my comfort zones.

God can help me take each step when the time comes. Here are some ideas about how God might help me—and how great it will feel to break through the layers:

_____

_____

WHAT'S THE BIG IDEA?

If you're going to get the sweetest fruit,
you're going to have to climb out on a limb.
Go for it!

Day 13
Divine Appointments

Always be ready to answer everyone who asks you
to explain about the hope you have.
But answer in a gentle way and with respect.
Always feel that you are doing right.

1 Peter 3:15–16 icb

Anthony had his mind totally on basketball last Saturday, but God had other plans.

Actually, Anthony was concentrating on hook shots and little else. He wanted to be on top of his game for the basketball tournament the next week. So he practiced on the court at the park. He was totally absorbed in shooting and rebounding when another kid walked up. It turned out his name was Pablo, and he wanted to play one-on-one.

Well, that wasn't really in Anthony's game plan for the afternoon. He was all about that hook shot. He stopped to think about it for a minute, and something about Pablo's shyness made Anthony agree. Clearly, it had taken a lot of courage for Pablo to come over and introduce himself.

So the pair played one-on-one for a while then took a breather. Anthony asked, "So, what's up? Where do you live?" And it didn't take long to learn that Pablo was going through a rough time. He had just moved to town and no one seemed friendly at all. "So what made you talk to me?" asked Anthony.

"The church name on the back of your shirt," said Pablo. "I don't go to church, but I thought maybe a church guy might be friendly."

Wow, thought Anthony, remembering he had almost said no. *Thanks for watching my back, Lord—literally!*

Anthony had asked God that morning to expand his borders, and it had happened, right there on the basketball court. A Jabez moment. The next day, Pablo was Anthony's guest at church, and they became friends. *Thanks, Lord.*

BREAKTHROUGH FACTS

I have Jabez moments like that all the time. So do my friends after they start using this prayer. And I don't have many boring days anymore. No matter where I am or what I'm doing, I always have one eye out to see who God will put in my path. I know it could happen anytime, anywhere.

It could happen to you, too—maybe tomorrow, maybe today. Are you ready for a Jabez moment—a divine appointment? If so, keep these five breakthrough facts in mind:

1. **Everyone has a need.** Jesus walked through a lot of crowds, and the Bible tells us He was moved with compassion. He looked out and saw so many people in need, and He knew He could help. You and I are standing in for Christ everywhere we go, and we've got to watch for those in need. Every person you meet is a Jabez encounter waiting to happen.

2. **God wants to use you now.** The problem is never God's ability to meet a need. It's your willingness to get involved. God once called, "Whom can I send? Who will go for us?" Isaiah looked left and right, and saw that nobody else was around. Who else could God be talking to? Then he got it. He said, "Here I am. Send me!" (Isaiah 6:8 ICB). If you could sneak a peek at God's daily planner, you'd see His divine appointment for you is *right now!* So you need to be in "heads-up" mode all the time.

3. **God's schedule for you is full of surprises.** I have days when God throws a Jabez moment to me, but I'm looking the

wrong way. It reminds me of when best friends sneak up from behind. Sometimes they'll cover our eyes and say, "Guess who!" We have to figure out the surprise. God sometimes wants us to "guess who" with our eyes open. Be on the lookout for your Jabez moment!

4. **Your main responsibility is being ready and open.** Here's something I pray all the time: "Lord, let me see what You want to do *in* me and *through* me today! Don't let me miss the big event!" You can't go anyplace where He doesn't have something in the works for you: on the basketball court, in the locker room, in the hallway at school, in the cafeteria—wherever. Here's your main clue: Anywhere there are people, there are needs.

ALWAYS **FEEL** THAT YOU ARE DOING **RIGHT.**

5. **Just ask, "How can I help you today?"** Then listen carefully. Kids will tell you their needs without even realizing they're doing it. Jesus was always asking questions. He knew it was a great way to get in a position to help someone. Ask yourself, *What can I do for this person?* God will show you a way. Just make that your slogan: "How can I help you today?"

Wherever you go today, keep this thought in mind: *God is at work right here, right now. I can help Him if I have a mind and a heart to do it. And wow, will that feel good!*

I'm absolutely convinced that today there's a miracle waiting with your name written all over it. Why not take a shot at it? Go for the slam dunk!

Day Thirteen

TALK BACK

Thinking back over the last couple of days, here are some Jabez moments that I missed:

Here are the places I go all the time where God might give me opportunities to help someone:

Lord, I want You to give me the ears to listen, the courage to say, "How can I help you today?", and the guidance to find a way to help as Jesus would. Here I'll write my prayer asking You to use me—and my promise that I'll be willing to help:

WHAT'S THE BIG IDEA?

*You can change a life in a minute—
if you let God be in it.*

Day 14
Taking the Plunge

"I know what I have planned for you," says the Lord.
"I have good plans for you. I don't plan to hurt you.
I plan to give you hope and a good future."

Jeremiah 29:11 ICB

IF YOU WANT TO CHANGE your life, you've got to start with your brain, right? You need a whole new way of thinking. And that new way of thinking comes straight from God's Word, the Bible.

Jesus said it this way: "You will know the truth. And the truth will make you free" (John 8:32 ICB). That means by fixing your mind on God's truth, which never changes, you are freed from the things that hold you back. Rewire your brain to God's way of thinking, and you become free to have cool adventures without fear.

For example, here's a truth you can latch onto: God wants you to have a bigger life and to do bigger things for Him.

Here's another one: God wants you to want that bigger life, those bigger opportunities to do things for Him, as much as He wants it for you. He wants you to ask Him for it every single day.

You don't have to have some huge feeling about it; you just have to be willing to ask! And that's something you can do every morning. Before you even get out of bed, take a moment and pray, "God, it's early and I'm still sleepy and maybe a little bit grumpy, but would You bring something or someone my way today? Would You give me an opportunity to enlarge my territory by helping somebody?"

God really likes it when we go to Him like that. It means we're not waiting for the right kind of feelings but depending on the right kind of thinking. We're letting the truth set us free.

It's Already Yours!

During our first week together, we found out that God really loves us and wants to make us happy. This week we've found that the best way for God to make us happy is to give us new ways to help people. Why? Because there's nothing in life that's more satisfying than

I PLAN TO GIVE YOU HOPE AND A GOOD FUTURE.

helping others. When we do that, we're doing what Jesus would do. And we're doing what God designed and put us on earth to do. No wonder it makes us so happy to serve others.

We've also seen that the greatest blessings are already ours—if we're willing to go get them. That means we have to move beyond our comfort zones. When God had great plans for His people in biblical times, here's what He said to them:

To Ruth: "It's already yours, but you have to leave your comfortable home and travel to a strange new place."

To Moses: "It's already yours, but you have to confront the leader, the Pharoah of Egypt—and become a leader yourself."

To Joshua: "It's already yours, but you have to fight for it."

To Esther: "It's already yours, but to claim it you must stand up for people who are in trouble."

Is God saying something like that to you today? Think of what you might accomplish—what might already be yours—if you're willing to trust God, step forward, and do the things you've been afraid to do. Sure, it's a little scary. But think about the facts. Is God good? Of course He is! Does He love you? Absolutely! Would He lead you wrong? Never! Will He help you take difficult steps? No doubt! Will He bless you for acting on faith? You'd better believe it!

Wrap your mind around those truths, then follow where they point you.

It's alread

LOOK OUT BELOW!

I know a teenager named Nick who took a vacation in Zimbabwe, Africa, with his dad. Dad thought hiking around Victoria Falls, the world's mightiest waterfall, would create great memories. But Nick had an idea for something even better: He wanted to jump off the skyscraper-high Victoria Falls Bridge—with his foot tied to a bungee cord!

Nick begged for permission. "C'mon, Dad!" he said. "That would make for a *huge* memory!" He pointed out that it was perfectly safe—well, mostly safe—and he could pay for it himself.

Dad inspected all the equipment, asked a lot of questions, and finally gave his permission. Nick paid for his ticket, strapped up—and took the plunge! When Nick let out that long, bloodcurdling yell, his dad nearly had a heart attack, but everything came out okay. In fact, Nick insisted on doing it a second time! That's living beyond the comfort zone, wouldn't you agree?

God's hand is more dependable than the best bungee cord. He'll never let you hit the bottom. The question is: Are you willing to take the plunge?

Think of how good you'll feel.

Think of how useful you will be.

Step out on the bridge of your faith, cling to God's hand, and take flight!

TALK BACK

Here are the most important truths I believe about God:

_____

_____

_____

Because I believe these truths, here are the actions they'll lead me to take:

_____

_____

_____

I can think of one little step I could take tomorrow. Here it is:

_____

_____

_____

WHAT'S THE BIG IDEA?

A young bird begins with a little hop,
then a leap—and before long, it can fly!
Are you ready for a little hop?

Day 15
GOD'S POWER

For our gospel did not come to you in word only,
but also in power, and in the Holy Spirit and in much assurance.

1 THESSALONIANS 1:5 NKJV

THE FIRST TIME you went "swimming," it was probably in one of those kid-size backyard pools, strictly for toddlers. But then you graduated to the "big kids'" pool in the park, the one that seemed as wide as a football field. Can you remember easing down those steps, clinging nervously to a parent's hand?

Soon you were moving all around the shallow end, not even clutching the wall anymore, thinking, *Hey, this is fun!* Of course, there were still challenges: You could get splashed. You could slip and fall. But you quickly became comfortable.

Then you took your first swimming lessons and set your sights on the deep end. This one took an extra dose of courage, but eventually you eased out there, ducking under the divider rope and swimming into new territory. You just had to smile; you'd conquered the whole pool. But after a few moments, you found out something new: You were in over your head! You couldn't stand on your own two feet anymore because the water completely covered you. It took either power or support to stay afloat. When you ran out of energy for swimming or treading water, you needed a hand—someone to keep you from sinking.

That's how it is when you take on greater challenges for God. There's that first cool rush: "Hey, I made it!" Then you might feel like you're in completely over your head. You're overwhelmed. You've moved into deeper challenges. And you need God's hand on you.

A Helping Hand

Think about our friend Jabez. He asked God to bless him, and God did. All the good things Jabez received from God made him want to do more for his Lord, so he prayed, "Give me more territory! Give me more room to serve You." And God did. The time must have come when Jabez was shocked to see all his new territory, new responsibilities, and new challenges.

Uh-oh, he probably thought. *Is this really what I wanted?* Could Jabez really handle all this stuff? Things had been so much simpler back in the "shallow end" of life. But before he became desperate, Jabez turned to prayer again. And this is what he said: "Oh, . . . that Your hand would be with me" (1 Chronicles 4:10 NKJV).

At first glance, that may seem like a nice, polite thing to say in a prayer. But it means so much more! In the Bible, the image of the hand (or arm) of the Lord is another way of expressing God's mighty power and special presence. When we read words like, "The hand of God was on Judah" (2 Chronicles 30:12 NKJV), we know that God gave Judah special power to accomplish supernatural results.

The Bible tells us that in the early days of the Christian Church, the news about Christ spread miraculously. People trusted Jesus, and "the hand of the Lord" made it happen (Acts 11:21 NKJV). Actually, the hand of God is always active whenever people serve Him. As you and I get busy doing Jesus' work, we receive His power. Isn't that exciting?

You'll be amazed by what happens when you take on new challenges to serve Him. Just as spending time in the deep end of the pool will make you a stronger swimmer, doing more for God will make you stronger in your faith.

A Welcome Hand

When Jennifer learned that a sight-impaired woman lived several houses down, she couldn't get the woman, Miss Rolader, out of her mind. She finally decided that God wanted her to do something. A little nervously, she walked to the woman's house and introduced herself. Then she said, "Miss Rolader, I enjoy reading aloud. I was wondering if you'd like me to come and read to you during the afternoons."

Miss Rolader was delighted. She already enjoyed recordings of books, and she loved the idea of having someone to read the daily newspaper or latest magazine aloud to her. Jennifer visited Miss Rolader every day to read to her. But after a couple of weeks, she realized she had a new challenge. Her homework had begun to suffer because she was spending less time studying. She asked God what she should do. "Please help me keep up my grades without giving up my new friend," she prayed.

About this time, Miss Rolader expressed an interest in Jennifer's schoolwork. Jennifer quickly discovered that Miss Rolader knew all kinds of things about science and social studies—the very subjects that gave Jennifer the most trouble. Miss Rolader said, "I love hearing the newspaper, Jennifer, but I bet your schoolbooks would be just as interesting. Could you read to me from them? We could discuss what you're learning in school."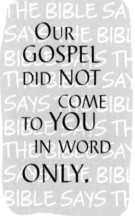

OUR GOSPEL DID NOT COME TO YOU IN WORD ONLY.

Jennifer takes her homework to Miss Rolader's house now, and the two friends are helping each other. That's how the hand of God reaches down to do something for us when we're doing something for Him. I hope you'll learn what Jennifer learned: God sends His miracles to those who do His ministry.

Day Fifteen

TALK BACK

Why not try your hand at an art project? Draw a rectangle below, and let it be the diagram of a swimming pool, as seen from above. Mark the shallow end and the deep end.

Got it? Now, in the deep end of your pool, write the name of a big new challenge that's hard for you to face. And put a little **X** close to the deep end but still in the shallow. That's you!

Now, draw a circle around the entire pool. Why? To show how big God is! Spend a few moments thinking about that as you look at your drawing. Then talk to God. Ask Him to help you to always remember that He's greater than any problem. And thank Him that life doesn't have to stay shallow!

WHAT'S THE BIG IDEA?

*God's awesome power begins
just where yours leaves off.*

ALLOW

DAY 16
NOT ABILITY, BUT AVAILABILITY

This is the message from the Lord to Zerubbabel:
"You will not succeed by your own strength or power.
The power will come from my Spirit,"
says the Lord of heaven's armies.

ZECHARIAH 4:6 ICB

DAN'S PARENTS had decided he was old enough to try baby-sitting, and Dan felt excited. For one thing, he could earn a little extra spending money. But it was also a chance to try something new for God. Dan had always enjoyed playing with children, and he saw this as a kind of ministry.

The Bannisters next door gave Dan his first shot at a real baby-sitting gig. They would only be gone for two hours while Dan watched Derek, a friendly four-year-old. Dan thought it would be a snap. He considered every crisis that might come up and knew, of course, that he could call Mom if things got crazy.

And things got crazy! As Dan poured Derek's fruit punch into a sippy cup, he spilled it on the counter. That red punch, he discovered, made a killer stain. While he was on the phone asking his mom what to do, Derek managed to pull a flower arrangement off the coffee table. Then Dan realized the fruit punch had gotten on Derek's clothing *and* the carpet.

When he finally got things cleaned up, Dan read to Derek from a book of children's Bible stories. But Derek didn't seem to hear a single word. He just giggled and ran around the room while Dan pointed to the colorful pictures. When Derek's parents returned, Dan tried to turn down the money—*He was a failure!*—but they insisted on paying him.

A week later, Mr. Bannister called Dan. "Can you help us again?"

"I can't believe you'd ask me," said Dan. "I thought I botched it!"

"Are you kidding?" asked Mr. Bannister, surprised. "Derek asks for you every day. And he keeps bringing us that Bible storybook you read to him. It's the only book he wants to hear. You've made the Bible fun for a four-year-old!"

Just Be There

THE POWER WILL COME FROM MY SPIRIT.

Dan discovered something we all find out eventually: We often don't realize how God is using our efforts. We always think we need to be experts with excellent talents to be of use. We believe we can't make a single mistake. But if that were true, nothing would ever get done. (And what would we need God for?)

He wants us to depend on Him. Sure, you'll have times when you feel like Dan, hopelessly overcome by the size of your new responsibilities. But then you'll be surprised to discover that God was there, using everything you offered, even when your efforts didn't seem successful to you. It's not your *abilities* that matter to Him; it's your *availability*. The power of God is working through you in ways you won't even realize.

I found a story of a Bible character who learned this same lesson. His name was Zerubbabel, and talk about overwhelmed! He had to contend with a mess far worse than the one in the Bannisters' living room. He led the first group of Israelites back to their homeland after it had been totally trashed. For many years, the Israelites had been slaves in another land. When Zerubbabel led them home, they found their city in ruins.

God asked Zerubbabel to build a new temple out of the shattered remains of the old one. But the request seemed impossible. Everyone was so discouraged that a huge rebuilding job seemed out of the question.

But it wasn't impossible at all. "You will not succeed by your own strength or power. The power will come from my Spirit," said God (Zechariah 4:6 ICB). In other words, "This isn't about your strength, Zerubbabel. It's about Mine." And in the next verse, God gives this example: "No mountain can stand in Zerubbabel's way. It will be flattened."

MOUNTAIN MOVERS, INC.

Wow! Our puny muscles may not be able to do much heavy lifting, but our God can turn a mountain into a parking lot, just like that! Think about it. God says to you and me, "Here, I'd like you to move a mountain!" Then He adds, "Oh, and remember, you're not strong enough to move a mountain." Finally, God says, "You and I will move the mountain together: My strength, your hands."

When you feel as if you have the strength and talent to do great things on your own, God isn't likely to use you. In fact, you're probably heading for a fall. But when you feel weak, discouraged, and overwhelmed, that's the very moment God can use your hands.

Might God be using you right now through your friends and activities? Don't think in terms of your ability, but rather your availability. Ask Him to use you—even when you don't know how He will do it!

TALK BACK

Now when I think of my friends and my activities, I realize God might use the things I say and do—without my realizing it—in the following ways:

_____

_____

_____

That word *available* seems very important. Here are some ways I can make myself more available to God:

I want more of God's power. I'm asking Him to use me today, tomorrow, and all week. I can't wait to see how He does it! Right here and right now, I'm going to tell God how I feel about Him:

WHAT'S THE BIG IDEA?

It's not the power of a person of God—
it's the power of God in the person.

Day 17
The Whole Ticket

I am the Lord. I am the God of every person on the earth.
You know that nothing is impossible for me.
JEREMIAH 32:27 ICB

YOUR BIRTHDAY PRESENT from Uncle Al was cool in the extreme, as usual. Uncle Al is retired, and he loves spending his money on gifts. And you like to receive gifts. So it works out nicely.

This year Uncle Al gave you an all-summer pass to the new amusement park. Everyone's been raving about this place, which supposedly has the most awesome rides in the galaxy. They say after spending a day there, someone has to practically pour your body into a container and ship it back home. It's that wild! And you get to go there *all summer*. One word, two syllables: In-tense.

On your first trip, you showed your pass and sprinted through the gates, heading for the big one: Moby Coaster! But the ticket taker at the turnstile held you back. He said your pass wasn't good for that ride. No way! Disappointed, you headed to the next ride, the one that shakes, rattles, and rolls your stomach. Again, you couldn't get through the turnstile. "But I've got an unlimited pass!" you argued. The ticket taker tried to tell you Uncle Al bought you a cheap ticket that only lets you into the park. No rides!

You knew that was wrong. And you quickly straightened out the problem at the park office. They issued you the wrong ticket, that's all. Uncle Al would never go cheap on you. You know him well enough to realize that. With the corrected pass, you take off again for the Moby Coaster.

The question is: Do you trust God as much as you trust Uncle Al? If you know the Lord well, you know that everything He gives you is the best. But for some reason, a lot of kids believe these lies about God:

- He only wants to bless them a little bit—just the "cheap" ticket.
- He has a plan for them, but it's no big deal—just a walk around the park.
- God won't really give them much power—there are no cool results involved.

You see, we *say* all the right things about God. But what we really need to do is believe the things we say. If we could do that, we'd stop all the walking around and start having all the thrills.

GOD IN A BOX

Some people keep God "in a box." What does that mean? When we keep God in a box our thoughts about Him are small and neat, and we keep them locked up. It's like your collection of CDs. Let's say you keep your music in a zippered CD case. You can slide the case into a drawer and forget about it, and the CDs will just sit there. There won't be any music unless you get that case out and open it.

But God isn't like that. He is alive. He is powerful. He doesn't fit into any box, and He constantly uses His power. He's working in your life whether or not you're thinking about Him. And missing out on the wonderful things He's doing is like going to the amusement park without getting on a single ride. God is so intense, so full of surprises and delight and joyful adventures! There is no one in this galaxy like Him.

And you know what the best part is? You can be absolutely, totally involved with Him. You have the entire, deluxe, unlimited, all-year, all-rides-included ticket. God is so generous, so loving that He would never give you anything less than the best. Getting to know God is sort of like exploring an amusement park that stretches to infinity and beyond. No matter how far you walk, you'll never be able to sample every wonderful new thing about God. There's always more. Your relationship with God just keeps getting better and better the more you serve Him.

WHO'S ROCKING THE BOAT?

While we're talking about intense, stomach-churning rides, let's remember that wild ride the disciples took. It happened on a boat when Jesus wasn't with them. He'd sent them on ahead while He prayed. Now several of these guys were fishermen, so they were used to getting tossed around by the waves. Roller coasters wouldn't have bothered them. But this storm blew up around them with no warning, and things got rough. The disciples didn't know whether they were going to live or die.

Suddenly Someone came walking toward them across the water. Who could it be but Jesus? The storm was so bad and the disciples were so terrified, they thought Jesus was a ghost (Mark 6:49). Of course Jesus calmly climbed into the boat, stilled the storm, and taught His friends something about His power. *Everything* is in His control. God says, "Nothing is impossible for me" (Jeremiah 32:27 ICB).

Some people are like those disciples. They get so upset by the everyday problems around them that they don't even see Jesus, right in front of them, able to calm the most terrifying storms.

Will you trust Jesus totally? Will you come to understand that His power goes beyond infinity? I hope so, because it's the most intense and thrilling ride you can imagine.

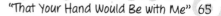

TALK BACK

I guess in some ways I've put God in a box. That is, I've never really realized just how much power He has. Here are some of the wrong ideas I've had about God:

But I'm thinking now about all the ways I can see His power in the world. Here are just a few:

I don't want to walk around the park without getting on any of the rides. I want to get involved with God! Here is how I can trust Jesus in my life:

WHAT'S THE BIG IDEA?

*God's power is too huge to understand
but too exciting to ignore.*

DAY 18
WHO'S GOT THE POWER?

"The Holy Spirit will come to you. Then you will receive power.
You will be my witnesses—in Jerusalem, in all of Judea,
in Samaria, and in every part of the world."

ACTS 1:8 ICB

DAKOTA WAS A TEENAGER when he first became serious about his faith. He still remembers the first time he felt God's power. God worked through him in an amazing way even though Dakota was "just a kid."

His church youth group had given a concert in a shopping center parking lot one afternoon when a woman walked up and began asking questions about God. Dakota stepped up to answer her questions. He hadn't been a believer for very long. He was a shy teenager who didn't talk much to adults or even to the other kids in the group. But there he was, handling the tough questions like an expert!

Dakota remembers how the other kids gathered around him later, their mouths hanging open. They wanted to know where he'd learned all that stuff and how he'd learned to say it so well. But Dakota felt just as surprised as they did. He shrugged and said, "I don't know. It was as if someone else jumped in and began speaking for me."

I've heard stories like this one many times. When people have such an experience, two things happen: They feel nervous and scared while it's happening, then they later realize that God was at work in them.

When you think about it, that kind of thing shouldn't happen just once in a lifetime. After all, God wants to use us. How else will He speak to people who need to hear His voice? Sure, His voice could roll from the sky through the hallways of your school: "Hey!

You down there! I'm God, and I want you to trust Me!" But God doesn't work that way. He doesn't send e-mails, either. Why should He do everything Himself? He'd much rather work with us!

I'LL DO THE TALKING

There's a great little story in Luke 21:12–15. Jesus told the disciples how God would use them to tell people about Himself. As His friends, Jesus said, they would be brought into the presence of kings. God planned to take advantage of those opportunities. "Don't worry about what you will say," Jesus told them. "I will give you the wisdom to say things so that none of your enemies will be able to show that you are wrong" (vv. 14–15 ICB).

It's amazing how that works. Just read the Book of Acts. Only a few weeks earlier, while Jesus was on trial as a criminal, Peter had been afraid to admit He was Jesus' follower. Three times he denied any knowledge of Jesus. But Acts 2 tells the story of how, after God's Spirit had come to the disciples, Peter preached about Jesus everywhere he went. Whenever he opened his mouth about the Lord, he became awesome with words! In fact, all of Jesus' disciples became different people as they went out into the world to tell others about Him.

YOU WILL BE MY WITNESSES IN EVERY PART OF THE WORLD.

It isn't just a Bible thing. It's true for you, too. Dakota certainly found that out. Acts 1:8 explains it to us simply: God's Spirit and all of His power dwell within us. When we depend upon His power, we will have courage and boldness to tell the world about Jesus.

PLUGGED IN AND READY FOR SERVICE

It's funny how you don't think much about your home's electrical service until a big storm comes along. Then the lightning flashes, the power goes out, and the whole house gets dark: no television, no stereo, and no computer! You'd forgotten how much you depended on that power current, hadn't you?

Isn't it a great moment when the electricity surges silently through the walls once more and the lights flicker back on? All the power you need is again available. The hair dryer works, the micro-wave heats food, and your computer files are available again. There's enough power for all of those things. You just plug them into the current, and the power flows through.

God's power works in a similar way. It's there for service and ministry, and it flows through us when we do the work God wants us to do. When you find yourself talking to others about Jesus, you'll realize the power is turned on. That's when God gives you extra strength and ability to speak for Him. Without God's power, we'd be like a house with no electricity.

We don't need to be afraid of God's power. And we don't need to be afraid to serve Him. God will give us courage, and He'll send His power surging through us to help others in need. He'll help us talk. He'll help us work. He'll help us know what to do in tough situations.

God has all the power you need.

PLUGGED IN

Day Eighteen

TALK BACK

I think the main reason that God insists on working through us, instead of doing everything Himself, is:

When I think about God using me to tell others about Him, here is how I honestly feel:

I want to know what it's like to serve God with His power, and I hope He'll use me soon. I'm going to tell Him how I feel about that right now:

WHAT'S THE BIG IDEA?

God's power is stronger than electricity.
Let it flow through you.

Day 19
BRAVE AND BOLD FOR GOD

God did not give us a spirit that makes us afraid.
He gave us a spirit of power and love and self-control.

2 TIMOTHY 1:7 ICB

TYLER DIDN'T HAVE A CLUE how to handle it. But it was a problem every day of his life. All he could do was stare at the floor, do as they told him, and hope it didn't last long.

Tyler was small for his age—thin, too. So he became an easy target for the bigger kids. Several times they teased him until he nearly cried. And they would absolutely have loved to see him cry. It was one of their goals. They waited for him every day by his locker. Some days they knocked his books on the floor, let him pick them up, and knocked them down again. Other days they made fun of his clothes or anything else that came to mind. They always poked and jabbed. Tyler just bowed his head, stifled his rage, and endured it alone.

Alone, that is, until David found out about the bullies. David had been asking God to show him what Jesus would do in his place. But when he heard about Tyler's problems, David responded automatically. He became so angry that he had to ask God to keep him from overreacting and doing something crazy.

The next time the big kids waited to pick on Tyler, they discovered David as well. They didn't really pay much attention to him, because David was small, too. But as soon as the bullying began, David stepped right in the middle of the big kids. "What's *your* problem?" asked the biggest one.

"I was about to ask you the same thing," replied David, looking him right in the eye.

"We're just messin' with our man Tyler here," said another boy.

"Then I guess you'll have to mess with both of us," David answered. He did not make threats. He simply stood beside his friend. It's called *solidarity*.

By that time, a little crowd had formed. Another kid suddenly stepped out of the crowd. David had never seen him before, but this other kid stood strong next to David and told the bullies, "Make that three of us." Tyler, David, and the new kid stood there until the bullies rolled their eyes and wandered away.

Surprised, David asked himself, *When did I become so bold?*

SUPERNATURAL COURAGE

Yesterday we discovered that God's Spirit gives us power. He also gives us boldness. The early Christians were incredibly bold, spreading their faith right under the noses of the Romans who had crucified their Savior. You'll find that word *bold* all through the Book of Acts—four times in the fourth chapter alone!

The first believers were no different from you or me. They simply said, "What would Jesus do in our place?" And they discovered that living with that idea changes everything. Soon they found themselves traveling to different countries and telling everyone they could find about Jesus. They kept going even when things became dangerous. They did it even when first-century bullies surrounded them.

HE GAVE US A SPIRIT OF POWER.

One of those early Christians was a young guy named Timothy. He was quiet and shy. And when he became a Christian, he remained the same old Timothy. But he became bold when his friend Paul encouraged him. "God did not give us a spirit that makes us afraid," the apostle Paul wrote to Timothy in a letter.

"He gave us a spirit of power and love and self-control" (2 Timothy 1:7 ICB). Eventually timid Timothy became the leader of the largest church of his time.

Power, love, and self-control. He sounds to me a little like David, the student who took a stand for his friend. Being a Christian doesn't make you a wimp. It does just the opposite! As long as you're doing the things that Jesus would do, God gives you power and makes you bold.

REALLY THERE

Imagine you're visiting heaven. There's Jesus, smiling and happy to see you. Even though He already knows everything about you, He asks, "What's up with you?" He's interested in how things are at home, how you're getting along with your parents and siblings. He asks about school and about your friends. As you bring Him up to date, you remember something you've wanted to tell Him. "I helped two of my friends end a huge argument," you say. "It was really hard for me to get in the middle of it, but we managed to make things peaceful again."

Jesus smiles. "Yes, I remember."

You're a little puzzled. "You mean You were there that day?"

And Jesus says, "I'm always with you, of course. But there are certain times when I'm there in a more powerful way. When you speak in love to make peace, when you help the hurting, when you offer a hand to the struggling—when you do any of these things, you can always be certain I'm right there beside you." He raises a hand with two fingers crossed tightly together. "Those are the times when you and I are just like this."

TALK BACK

Have there been times lately when I could have been bolder? Was there someone I might have helped this past week? Here's what I remember:

I realize that God will make me bold. I only have to be willing to do something for Him. Right here, right now, I'm going to ask God to give me that chance:

There's a person I know who needs my encouragement. Here's something nice I'm going to do for that person this week:

WHAT'S THE BIG IDEA?

God's power makes me bold
and makes anything possible.

DAY 20
NO PRIDE INSIDE

The people saw this and were amazed.
They praised God for giving power like this to men.
MATTHEW 9:8 ICB

"YOU SHOULD BE PROUD of yourself!" Kimi had heard those words so many times, they finally came true.

Kimi belonged to a club for girls. The girls did a number of activities, some just for fun, and some to help the community. One day they visited a retirement home. The older folks who lived there really enjoyed the girls' visit. And so did the girls—particularly Kimi. Her grandparents lived thousands of miles away. She hadn't seen them in years. Perhaps her grandparents were like these gentle, smiling people.

Kimi continued to ride her bike to the center for visits, even without the rest of her club. She had fun and felt good about serving God. Her parents thought she had a wonderful thing going. Kimi often brought little gifts or things the residents needed, and they did things for her, too. The women taught her to play a new card game. The men told stories of the old days.

Then the editors of the local newspaper heard about Kimi's visits. They thought her dedication to her new friends would make a nice, heartwarming story, so they printed an article, complete with pictures. Kimi hadn't expected this. It made her feel kind of famous, really. The girls' club gave her a special award, and so did her school. "You should be proud of yourself," everyone said.

Kimi enjoyed all the praise. She began to think of how much fun it might be if the newspaper wrote *another* story about her.

There had been a lot of talk about the ugly litter over in the park. Maybe she could go over and pick up trash. If she did this on a Saturday, plenty of people would see her. Maybe someone would call the newspaper, and she could be back in the spotlight.

As Kimi planned her Saturday, she didn't even realize she'd stopped visiting the retirement home. The people there grew sad, missing their young friend. Kimi had forgotten all about them.

LEAVE THE PRIDE OUTSIDE

Dealing with pride is difficult, isn't it? We love hearing people say nice things about us. When our parents and teachers reward us for doing the right thing, we're encouraged to be better people.

But when we serve God, we can't forget to give Him the credit. *He* gave us the power to do good things. *He* gave us the love for others. If we begin to think we're something special, it changes the way we serve God. Kimi focused on helping the people in the retirement home, at first. Everyone got simple pleasure and joy out of her visits. But pride got involved, and soon her focus wasn't about serving God and people anymore. It became about Kimi—and about receiving people's praise.

Pride gets in our way of being God's partners. We start thinking of ourselves instead of Him. We don't hear Him whispering to us anymore, telling us what He would like us to do. We spend too much effort trying to look good to others. .

You'll know God's truest friends when you meet them because they won't be puffed up with pride. They won't seem conceited or concerned with themselves. They'll pay attention to *you*. They'll listen carefully, without interrupting.

POINTING UPWARD

Moses was one of the greatest men to ever serve God, and God loved him deeply. But Moses made an awful mistake. His story shows how serious it is to become conceited and to try to grab God's glory.

Moses was leading his people through the desert. God told him to speak to a big rock, and He would cause water to flow from it miraculously. But Moses chose to do things his way. Instead of *speaking* to the rock, he grumbled to the people, "Must we bring water for you out of this rock?" (Numbers 20:10 NKJV). Then he *struck* the rock with his walking stick. The water came gushing out, but there was a problem. First, Moses hadn't followed God's instructions. And did you notice that Moses used the word *we*? That showed what was inside his mind: Moses thought he had power to bring water from a rock. Moses' proud behavior broke God's heart. As much as He loved Moses, God punished him by not allowing him to enter the Promised Land. We can all learn from that painful but necessary lesson. Always give God the credit.

There's a guy named Josh who does just that. He says a little prayer both before and after everything he does for God. Even if he's raking leaves for his parents, he thanks God for giving him the chance to be useful. That little prayer changes his whole attitude, even about raking leaves! Then, after he's finished, he quietly whispers, "Thanks, God!"

THE PEOPLE SAW THIS AND WERE AMAZED.

Josh's friends have all noticed his habit of holding up his forefinger, as if he's pointing at the sky whenever someone comments on a job he's done well. They know what he means: "Don't give me the glory. It's all about Him!"

TALK BACK

Okay, I admit it. I've gotten a little "puffed up" before. Here's an example:

I'm starting to understand that God deserves the glory for everything I do. Here's why I believe that is true:

I need a handy way of thanking God and giving Him the credit for good things I do. Here's how I'll do it:

WHAT'S THE BIG IDEA?

Don't let pride get in the way.
Give the glory to God.

DAY 21
IT'S REAL . . . TODAY

The "right time" is now. The "day of salvation" is now.
2 CORINTHIANS 6:2 ICB

MATT AND MARK FOUGHT CONSTANTLY. This didn't surprise anyone, because they're brothers only a year apart. They loved each other, of course, but they always competed. If the family headed for the car, they raced for the front seat. No matter who got there first, an argument always followed.

Everyone got a little tired of hearing these quarrels. Finally, the church softball coach sat them down for a talk (not that Mom and Dad hadn't tried several thousand times). "So, do you guys enjoy fighting?" asked the coach.

Matt and Mark looked at each other then back at the coach. "Um, no, sir," they stammered, almost in unison.

"If your lives depended upon it—if your next argument caused you both to drop dead—do you think you could get through a day without arguing?"

"Yes, sir."

"Of course!"

"Then I guess you could stop fighting if you really wanted to, huh?" the coach continued. "What about God? Do you think He enjoys your arguments?"

Matt and Mark looked at the dirt beside the bench. "Um, no, sir."

"Do you think He wants you to treat each other with respect, love, and true friendship?"

They looked up, surprised by his question. "Yes, sir."

"Any reason you can't start obeying God right now?" Coach asked.

"No, sir. None at all," answered Matt.

"We're *on* it, sir," agreed Mark.

"If you really mean that," said the coach, "God will be pretty pumped about it, you know? He'll do everything, He can back you up, beginning right now. He'll make your friendship with each other *solid.* Just cooperate with God. You'll be tied together, best buddies for life. And guys, that's going to be a lot more fun than barking at each other!"

You could see those thoughts take hold. While the boys still struggle occasionally, they're trying harder to let God strengthen their relationship. And they've discovered that it is more fun to both be on the winning side.

Ready and Real

THE "RIGHT TIME" IS NOW.

Sometimes God's power seems, well, *out there.* Many people think it's something people had in ancient biblical times, just something we talk about in Sunday school. God's power seems so out there—not ready and real and available today.

But here's the real deal. God's power isn't for somewhere, someday. It's for right here, right now. Any moment when you want to please God, His power is like money in the bank. You can draw it out and use it as you need it. And the great thing is, you can never use it all up.

God eagerly waits for you to take advantage of His power. But how should you use it?

- God's power can help you break that bad habit—that behavior of yours that displeases Him. It can help you to stop arguing with your parents or siblings. It can help you to stop ignoring your responsibilities. It can win out over any bad habit you'd like to break.

℮ God's power can make you useful to Him and to other people. He supports your efforts to become a better servant. His power pours into the world through your service and help.

℮ God's power helps you spread the news that Jesus is Lord. God always strengthens us when we let the world know how we feel about Jesus.

Wouldn't you love to feel a new kind of power and excitement for God in your life? It can be yours right here, right now, even before you put this book down. It all depends on what you're attempting to do. If you're working to make God happy, His power is ready for action.

WHY WAIT?

I love this story from Acts 8. A Christian named Philip was walking along when the Spirit directed him to something interesting. A traveler from Ethiopia had pulled his chariot to the side of the road. He sat there puzzling over a scroll. Philip discovered the man was studying the Old Testament Scriptures, but he needed some help. So Philip began to explain the meanings to him.

Philip led the man to Christ right there on the road. Then the traveler said, "Look! Here is water! What is stopping me from being baptized?" (Acts 8:36 ICB). In other words, "Why wait? I want to experience God right here, right now!" God absolutely loves that attitude. He wants us to come running into His arms with tremendous excitement. He wants us to be as thrilled to be with Him as He is to be with us.

Why WAIT?

Day Twenty-one

TALK BACK

Today I learned that God's power is a "right now" kind of thing. I'm not sure I've thought about that before. Here's what I've always thought about God's power:

As I went through today's reading, one particular bad habit of mine came to mind. It's something I know God's power can help me beat, and here's what it is:

As I trust God to help me do something special for Him tomorrow. Right here, right now, I'll write down some ideas about what that might be:

WHAT'S THE BIG IDEA?

God's power is for now, this minute.
You can live in it this instant!

DAY 22
DON'T EVEN GO THERE!

Do not lead us into temptation, but deliver us from the evil one.
MATTHEW 6:13 NKJV

WE'VE LEARNED A LOT about God's plan for us, haven't we? We've seen that God loves to bless us with His goodness. We've seen that blessings lead us to ask Him for more ways to serve Him. But then we need more of His power to handle more of His work.

There's one more big idea in this amazing prayer.

Like Jabez, we've discovered that once we're given new territory for God's work, we face new struggles. We're taking something from the devil and giving it to God. When that happens, the devil always fights back by tempting us to do something wrong. That behavior (the Bible calls it *sin*) will ruin any chance we have of making a difference for God.

So, the final portion of Jabez's prayer is about asking God to keep us away from evil. Jesus closed the Lord's Prayer the same way. Just like Jabez, Jesus prayed, "Do not lead us into temptation, but deliver us from the evil one." Both prayers say, "Wherever evil is, keep me on the other side of the world!"

It's a simple prayer, but it works. "Lord, steer me clear of the bad stuff!"

FILE DELETED

Let's say you have a video game on your computer that's hard to resist. Mega-Mutilation 3 makes you a robot that shoots down innocent people—complete with blood and gore—as you rampage through the streets with evil intent. The game distracts you and keeps you from getting your homework done. You're sure God wants you to do more positive and productive things than play Mega-Mutilation 3 anyway. So how will you change things?

1. By leaving the game on your computer and asking God to help you resist it.
2. By deleting the game files from your computer's drive.

If you answered 2, you pass the test! Leaving the game on your hard drive just invites more rounds of temptation. Why give the devil those opportunities?

If you keep tripping over the skates you left on the floor of your bedroom, you don't need to ask God to help you walk more carefully. You need to reach over, pick up the skates, and put them away. Make sense? When you're doing more for God, you need to ask Him to keep evil as far away as possible.

OUT OF THE LINE OF FIRE

Palo learned this lesson painfully. He has had three best buddies since kindergarten. Since they were little, the group has called itself the Fantastic Four. They've had dozens of sleepovers and celebrated all their birthdays together. Despite being assigned to different classes in school, they've stayed tight.

But in the last year or so, the group has changed—or Palo has.

The FF (Fantastic Four) has always been all about a good laugh. But recently Palo has sensed that the laughter has grown sort of sarcastic. He and his three buds have started hanging out in the hall and tossing wisecracks at certain kids who walk by. Whenever the four get together, they mostly snicker and criticize. The FF suddenly doesn't seem so fantastic anymore to Palo. He doesn't like the way he behaves, or feels, when he's with his friends.

A few weeks ago Palo saw James, a not-very-athletic kid, struggling in gym class. James couldn't finish the half-mile the class was supposed to run. As he stopped to walk—huffing and puffing—kids zoomed by him, muttering sarcastic comments as they passed. Palo cruised up beside James, clapped him on the shoulder, and said, "C'mon, man. You and I are going to finish this thing together, okay?" And with Palo's encouragement, James picked up his feet and began to run with new spirit. Palo liked helping someone else become more and do more.

That same afternoon while the Fantastic Four were hanging out, one of them started making fun of a kid coming toward them. Palo looked up and recognized James. He'd obviously wanted to talk to Palo, but the ridicule caused him to turn around and leave. Palo suddenly felt about two inches tall.

He thought long and hard after the James incident. He saw himself living in two worlds: his old, easy world of the Fantastic Four and his new world of serving God. The new one required him to live in a different way, with higher standards. And people were watching. He didn't want them to think the Christian life was about sarcasm and insults.

Palo wondered if God wanted him to work on cleaning up the group's act. Maybe his friends would drop all the snickering stuff if he asked them to. But deep down, he knew that wasn't going to happen. It was much easier for three guys to change Palo than the other way around.

Deliver Us From The Evil One.

Today Palo still considers the other three in the Fantastic Four his friends. He just avoids hanging out with them as a group. He won't let himself drift into that attitude. God wants better things from him.

And you know what? God has given him plenty of new friends.

Day Twenty-two

TALK BACK

I can understand why people who serve God face temptation every-where they go. Here's my take on that:

There have been times when I've felt tempted to do something I knew God didn't want me to do. This recent incident is an example:

Here's the best way I know to come out on top when I feel tempted:

WHAT'S THE BIG IDEA?

When temptation comes to town,
it's best to shop for a new zip code.

Day 23
Finding the Emergency Exit

The only temptations that you have are the temptations that all people have. But you can trust God. He will not let you be tempted more than you can stand. But when you are tempted, God will also give you a way to escape that temptation. Then you will be able to stand it.

1 Corinthians 10:13 icb

IMAGINE YOU'RE SITTING in your front yard. A stranger rides by on his junky old motorcycle, all dirty and dressed in black. He's reading the numbers on the mailboxes. When he comes to yours, he stops. This makes you a little nervous because he's one evil-looking dude. You hide behind a tree and watch to see what happens.

The stranger walks to the door and rings the bell. What could this stranger want with your family? You're thinking of shouting out a warning, but the door is quickly opened—by Jesus!

"Excuse me," says the stranger hesitantly. "Isn't this the home of—?" And he says your name.

Jesus quietly replies, "Yes it is. But My friend has asked Me to watch the door."

The stranger scowls impatiently. For a moment, you think he's going to try to power his way in. But then the stranger's eyes fall on the nail-scarred hand on the doorknob. He looks up to the thorn marks on Jesus' head. The devil—for that's who he is—snarls, climbs on his motorcycle, and rides away.

> **HE WILL NOT LET YOU BE TEMPTED MORE THAN YOU CAN STAND.**

That's not just a fantasy. It's a vivid word picture for you to remember whenever you face temptation. When you ask Him to, Jesus guards the door of your heart and makes the devil hit the highway. Hebrews 2:18 tells us that Jesus had to handle temptation Himself, so He knows how we feel. He won out over it once, and He can stand at your heart's door and help you win, too. Cool, huh?

This is another part of Jesus' amazing power within us. Yesterday we discovered that the best way to avoid evil is simply to stay out of its way. But sometimes temptation comes looking for us. And when we hear it knocking, it's always good to send Jesus to the door. We do that by remembering He has power over every kind of sin that might tempt us.

LOOK FOR THE EXIT

Here's another incredible fact. You might call this one the glowing exit sign. Have you ever entered a dark movie theater and felt completely blind? You think, *I can't see a thing! How can I find a seat without accidentally sitting on someone's lap?* Then you see a little sign glowing in the dark, way down in the corner. You see four red letters: E-X-I-T. After that, your eyes slowly grow accustomed to the dark. You begin to make out which seats have people in them and which ones don't. It's also nice to know that if you have to get out of that theater quickly—say, in case of a fire—you can find those glowing letters easily. What a relief!

The verse at the beginning of today's reading says that every time you find yourself in a dark spot, you can look for the glowing exit sign. Yes, according to 1 Corinthians 10:13, God will always provide "a way to escape" from the temptation before you. The verse also says God won't ever let you run into a temptation tougher than you can handle.

So, we know these two things:

1. No matter how big the temptation is, God is bigger.
2. No matter how dark things look, there's always a right way out.

I've used that verse repeatedly in my own life to deal with temptation. Let's say I'm really feeling pulled to do something I know is wrong. First, I recognize what it is: a temptation to *sin*. (It's important to call it by its name.) Second, I say this out loud: "This temptation of (insert the problem here) is *not* too strong for me, because God promised He would keep it small enough for me to handle right this minute!"

That strategy helps a lot. But I'm not finished. I also say, "God told me He'd provide a door out of this dark moment. I'm going to look around until I *see* it." And soon I find something I can do that will help me. I just look around for that glowing exit sign.

Once I've called the temptation by its true name, I shine God's light on it. Sin never likes the light, and it scampers for dark corners. Suddenly I realize I don't *have* to give in to it. Now, in the light, I can see the sin for what it is: a puny, pathetic little thing that tried to trip me up in the dark.

That's how I try to stop any temptation right in its tracks, so I won't be bothered by it again! I hope you'll do the same.

Day Twenty-three

TALK BACK

I've never thought of Jesus guarding the door of my heart. Here's how that word picture makes me feel:

The temptation I face most often is the one I'm about to write. And I'll bet I can think of the exit sign, too, and write the way to avoid it:

This is a good time to think about what causes problems in my life and how Jesus guards me from these temptations. I can list three ways to avoid them:

WHAT'S THE BIG IDEA?

When we're tempted, we must choose between two doors. One leads to victory. The other leads to a thousand more dark doors.

Day 24
Turning the Tables on Temptation

It is the evil that a person wants that tempts him.
His own evil desire leads him away and holds him.

JAMES 1:14 ICB

IMAGINE YOU WENT to school early one day to finish off your homework. You opened the door of an empty classroom. Someone was already there: a creepy guy with his back to you, talking to himself and scribbling notes. You did a double take—didn't you hear him say your name?

Yep. That was old Lucifer in the empty room, and he was planning the temptations he was going to use on you that day. He didn't know you were there. As you listened, you heard his plans. He'd get you to daydream during math. He'd slip you some prime gossip between classes. He'd nudge you into an argument with your parents and get you to raise your voice at them at dinner. Throughout the day, you could always stay on the high road and please God. But the devil hoped to cut you off at every pass.

You closed the door quietly. How did you go through that day, after hearing the devil's plans? My guess is that you didn't go down easy. You prepared yourself for every little temptation. You had a few surprises of your own for the Dude of Darkness.

The cool thing about this story is that you can make it come true, just like yesterday's story. The devil's plans aren't exactly advanced algebra. Just sit down with a piece of paper and a pencil; I'll bet you can quickly name the devil's top two or three strategies for tripping you up. The devil is very systematic in his work. He finds out what works and sticks with it.

TAKE THE TEST

Why not get that piece of paper right now? Write the numbers from one to five and answer these questions:

1. Which day of the week do I sin most often?
2. What time of day do I sin most often?
3. Where do I sin most often?
4. Who am I with when I sin the most?
5. Which sins do I commit most often?

The devil has already made a similar list of questions with your name on it. His list asks, Which day do I get the biggest sin from this person? What time? Where? Who? Which?

Now let's add two more questions to *your* list:

6. How do I usually feel just before I sin?
7. What kinds of thoughts do I usually have *as* I sin?

As you move through life, you'll find unhealthy feelings can push you toward unwise behavior. Like, if you're jealous of someone, you might gossip about him or her. And as you gossip, you might think your words will make someone else dislike the person you're jealous of. That's an idea the devil promotes. But you can beat him at his game. Just figure out his next his move. Then be ready.

CAUGHT IN THE ACT

Kiah and her mom were fighting a war, battle by battle. Kiah remembered all the good times she'd once had with her mom: reading together, going to the circus, building a doll collection. Why couldn't they be friends anymore?

What could Kiah do to fix this relationship? She made a list like the one you made earlier. Then she had an idea. Why not pretend this whole thing was a word problem in her math book? She wrote this:

"Kiah has a problem with sin. It often happens on Saturday

evenings. It takes place at Kiah's home, usually in the kitchen or the living room, and involves a big argument with her mom. Just before the argument, Kiah usually feels that her mother is treating her like a child. She somehow tries to relieve this frustration by yelling at her mom. How many more arguments can Kiah and Mom have before they ruin their friendship?"

Kiah solved the problem quickly. The answer was zero.

As with all word problems, she could find the solution could be worked out by looking at the factors in the question. Kiah quickly realized she and her mom usually argued after spending the day together on Saturdays. Even when Kiah made plans for herself, her mom always seemed to interrupt them with chores or other requests. And if Kiah wanted to hang out at the mall or go to a movie with her friends, her mom always wanted to know exactly where she'd be and when she'd be home. It frustrated Kiah to feel babied and told what to do, and the sum total of her frustration was usually a loud battle.

IT IS THE EVIL THAT A PERSON WANTS THAT TEMPTS HIM.

Kiah had to cut off the path of temptation. Her main step: Talk to Mom about her feelings without yelling. Her mother was very eager to listen to her. Mom didn't like the arguing any more than Kiah did. She hadn't realized that Kiah and her friends never, ever separated at the mall or theater—not even for a moment. And Kiah learned that her mom's best friend had once had a very scary experience by herself in a movie theater. These kinds of revelations rarely happen when everyone is yelling. But once peace broke out, Kiah and her mom could begin to hear each other and move toward realistic solutions without the sin.

And don't you just know the devil was ripping up his battle plans and kicking himself!

Day Twenty-four

TALK BACK

I'd really like to know the devil's plans for making me stumble. For example, here are several ways that I know I allow sin to come into my life:

And here are several ways that I will work to cut off the path of temptation in my life:

WHAT'S THE BIG IDEA?

Always do your homework
before the devil hands you a test.

DAY 25
THE INSTANT TEMPTATION BUSTER

The Lord is the Spirit. And where the Spirit of the Lord is, there is freedom.
2 CORINTHIANS 3:17 ICB

CHEYENNE WASN'T SURE what her problem was. She was constantly making nasty little remarks about Mai. It always made her feel like a jerk, but she couldn't seem to stop.

What was the problem? Mai hadn't done anything to Cheyenne. Everyone seemed to like Mai. Well, that was part of the problem. Cheyenne was a little jealous of Mai. The guys all thought Mai was hot. Her parents were loaded, and she had all the best stuff. She was always going on skiing trips or inviting other kids to spend the weekend on the family's boat. She even got all the best awards at Honors Day.

Cheyenne wanted to be that popular. She wanted to have cool stuff and win a few awards. But she was only Cheyenne—*resentful* Cheyenne. Eventually someone would say, "Did you hear Mai's got a new skateboard?" Then Cheyenne would say something like, "Naturally. Ms. Wonderful owns it all." And everyone would turn and look at her funny.

Cheyenne prayed about it, but she realized her remarks always bubbled out of her mouth because of her anger. Even if she put duct tape over her mouth, what could she do about the feelings boiling inside her?

One day she told her older sister, Katie, about her problem. Her response totally floored her. She thought she'd lecture her about judging others, but instead she started flipping through her Bible. She showed her John 14:16–17 (ICB), where God said He would send us a *Helper*. "The Holy Spirit is there to help soothe those bubbling feelings," Katie said.

What a concept! Cheyenne went right back to her room and prayed. "Lord," she said, "whatever that hot lava is inside me, it's too hot for me to handle. Would You help me and, well, cool off my insides next time I want to make a nasty remark?"

God answered Cheyenne's prayer faster than she expected. Almost before she could open her eyes, Cheyenne felt the cool comfort of God's Spirit. And here's the message she felt: *Cheyenne, if you had any idea how much I love you, things would be different. If you could only love yourself as I love you, you wouldn't have to be jealous of anyone. I put a lot of work into making you. I gave you gifts and talents. I made only one Cheyenne. So relax. Let Mai be Mai, and you be Cheyenne. It will make a difference in how the other kids feel about you, too.*

GOD'S COMFORT

It's amazing how many incredible gifts God has given us, isn't it? How many have you learned about during your Jabez adventure?

Add this one to the list. When you're raging inside, God's Spirit will help and comfort you. All you have to do is ask. When you feel yourself coming close to sinning, talk to God about it. Think about the feelings that are pushing you to sin. What are you angry about? What's frustrating you? What will come from your sin? As you ask yourself those questions, the Spirit of God will help you sift through them.

He's so gentle, so loving. If you ever feel a little voice inside yelling at you, saying you're terrible, that's not the Spirit of God. It's just another bubble rising from the churning turmoil inside you. The Holy Spirit doesn't criticize. He helps. He comforts. He says, "Come on,

My friend, you don't want to do that, do you? You know you're better than that. You know it will cause pain for you and other people if you do that. Be strong this time. I'll help you."

God talks to you that way sometimes when you don't even know it's Him. He doesn't make a big deal about it. He just gently encourages you and eases the troubling feelings that disrupt your life. So why not call on Him for help? Why not ask for His comfort and reassurance? If you can do that, you'll have a surefire way to avoid temptation.

WHERE THE SPIRIT OF THE LORD IS, THERE IS FREEDOM.

THREE MINUTES TO GOD'S VICTORY

I've used this method repeatedly: I've caught myself thinking about doing something I shouldn't do, and I've asked God to send His comfort to my aching heart.

You know what? God has answered my prayer every single time. Every now and then, I even take off my watch and time it! Usually within three minutes, I begin to feel peaceful inside. It's not as if I can tell exactly when it happens, but all the churning ceases. God comforts me, and then the last thing I want to do is sin against Him.

Ask God to help you understand exactly what causes the unhappy feelings inside you. Talk to your parents and siblings. Bring them all out of the darkness and into the light. You'll see them much more clearly. You'll know you can overcome these feelings. And the next time temptation comes, you'll know the Spirit is there to soothe you.

THREE MINUTES TO God's Victory
Day Twenty-five

TALK BACK

I realize that sin often begins with negative feelings inside me. I can think of a time just this week when that happened. Here's what I felt, and here's what I did:

Here is the temptation that gets me most often, and here's why I think it happens:

I'm going to ask God right now to help me remember to seek His help and comfort when I'm tempted to give in to that sin:

WHAT'S THE BIG IDEA?

Calm the inside of a volcano and it becomes a beautiful, majestic mountain.

DAY 26
BEAST ON THE PROWL

Control yourselves and be careful! The devil is your enemy.
And he goes around like a roaring lion looking for someone to eat.
Refuse to give in to the devil. Stand strong in your faith.
1 PETER 5:8–9 ICB

LIONS ONCE LIVED IN ISRAEL. They roamed the desert, the mountains, and the thickets along the rivers. David the giant-slayer knew what it was like to kill a lion. So did Samson. It took a hero to handle the "king of beasts."

Lions also prowled the Roman arenas. Emperor Nero released them inside the stadiums to attack Christian prisoners. Yes, early Christians had a healthy fear of lions. So when they wrote about the devil, they sometimes portrayed him as a hungry lion.

The devil is our enemy, and he's very real. You've seen cartoons that show him as a little man dressed in red with horns and a pitchfork. That's just how the devil would like you to think about him. If you see him as cute and having a pointy tail, you can't take him seriously. Well, don't expect to find that picture in the Bible. Instead, you'll find the more realistic image of a prowling, raging lion.

Not that you should tremble with fear when you think of the devil. Instead, picture him another way the Bible describes him, as a coward showing you his back. It's true. If you offer any resistance at all to his little act, he will turn around and run away! "Stand against the devil, and the devil will run away from you" (James 4:7 ICB).

Take him seriously? Absolutely. Fear him? No way. Someone more powerful stands by your side with greater power than the devil.

PRIMARY TARGETS

Yesterday we saw how the devil keeps it simple. He comes after you the same way every time. If you pay attention, you can predict his moves and prepare for his schemes.

The Bible tells us about a man named Nehemiah who wanted to rebuild the walls of Jerusalem. The whole city lay in ugly ruins. Nehemiah gathered a small army of men to go and rebuild the walls. But they were constantly surrounded by enemies who didn't want those walls rebuilt. The enemies did everything they could to threaten and distract Nehemiah's men. They played mind games, just as the devil does.

REFUSE TO GIVE IN TO THE DEVIL.

Nehemiah divided his men into two groups. One laid bricks while the other stood with weapons in hand, ready to defend their turf. After a while, the men changed places. They worked "from sunrise till the stars came out" (Nehemiah 4:21 ICB).

Sometimes, that's what it takes. You have to grit your teeth, gather strong friends, and stand firm. In the end, the victory will be yours because Jesus will be stronger than the devil every single time. It's simply a matter of controlling your feelings and having godly stubbornness.

A CLASS ACT

At one school, a snobbish group seemed to run everything. Most kids wanted to be part of the popular gang, so they looked up to that elite group. They imitated the snobbishness by focusing on the "right" kind of clothes. They learned to be cruel to anyone who didn't fit their system. And the school cranked out more and more snobs.

Jeremy knew this situation was wrong, and he wanted to make things different. He decided to run for class president. He told everyone that if he got elected, he'd try to create a school uniform policy so everyone could feel equal. He adopted a campaign slogan: Vote for an Equal Society.

Immediately Jeremy came under attack. The popular kids whispered about him, spreading false rumors. Jeremy's parents got prank phone calls at home. An obscene word was painted on his locker one morning, and his friends felt pressured to abandon him. Jeremy began to get a little discouraged.

Monday morning he arrived at school ready to drop out of the election. But he discovered a note shoved into the vent on his locker. *Oh, great. What is it this time?* he thought. He almost tossed it on the floor without reading it. But the first words caught his eye:

> Jeremy,
>
> Hang in there, man. If you give in, who else will step up? It takes guts to make a stand. We may be quiet but we're right behind you all the way. We want to help you make this school different. We're telling everybody we know to vote for you. Maybe we'll lose, but you gotta start somewhere, right? We're on our way. Two words: Solidarity. Hope.

Signatures filled the bottom of the page—lots and lots of them. Jeremy folded the note carefully and placed it inside his shirt, next to his heart. Nothing in the world could make him quit now.

I hope you'll feel this way as you stand firm for God. In the power of Jesus, every one of us can be a lion tamer.

A Class Act

Day Twenty-six

TALK BACK

It makes sense that the devil would target people who try to help God. Here's how that makes me feel:

I know Jesus is always stronger than the devil. Here are some ways I know He will help me whenever I feel tempted to give up:

I know I can count on these friends to watch my back when I'm trying to work for God:

WHAT'S THE BIG IDEA?

*The devil runs up fast when we serve God,
and runs away even faster when we trust God.*

Day 27
Keep up Your Guard

Doing what is right brings freedom to honest people.
But those who are not trustworthy will be caught by their own desires.

Proverbs 11:6 ICB

HARRY HOUDINI was the world's greatest escape artist. He could break out of any jail cell, bank vault, locked trunk, or chains. He was once suspended upsidedown by rope, chained, handcuffed, and lowered into a water tank. How could he possibly escape in time to get a breath of air? Though he was left for dead, he got out alive. Houdini's secret? He carefully developed his body and planned every detail of each stunt.

But one day he wasn't sufficiently prepared. Houdini had often challenged people in the audience to punch him in the stomach. Their hardest hits never hurt him because he carefully tightened his stomach muscles before each punch. But one day, a member of the audience walked up and, without any warning, socked Houdini twice in the stomach. The escape artist wasn't ready, and he suffered serious injuries. A few days later, Harry Houdini died.

A similar thing can happen in your life. It's unlikely that someone will put you away with a punch in the stomach, but there are other kinds of traps. The best way to escape from them is to always be prepared.

Taking It to the Next Level

Why should things be more "dangerous" when you're serving God?

The reason is that you've chosen to live on a whole new level. You've graduated to the "big leagues" of spiritual living. And you've dedicated yourself to bringing God's awesome blessings to this world. As soon as you step up to that higher level, new realities confront you:

- ℮ Your actions and decisions affect more people.
- ℮ Your unselfish service is more tiring.
- ℮ Your success causes you to relax and become overconfident.
- ℮ Your responsibilities to God grow more complicated.

DOING WHAT IS RIGHT BRINGS FREEDOM.

Like Harry Houdini, you'd better watch out! You're on the bigger stage now. You have to be prepared for tests that will appear unexpectedly.

What would you like to do for God? You're trying to serve Him the best you can in your home, at your school, and in all the places you go. People are going to know that being a Christian is very important to you. They'll realize you're serious about helping to make the world the kind of place God wants it to be. Even though it's not fair, some people expect God's partners to be perfect. In other words, they'll think you shouldn't ever make mistakes because you're connected to God. To test you, some people will look for your weak spot, just as the man who punched Houdini did.

Sure, you'll mess up now and then. It's bound to happen. The important thing is to use even your worst mistakes to make God look good! Is that possible? Sure. Let me tell you about my friend Namid.

UNSAFE AT HOME

Namid is one of those kids who feels excited about the prayer of Jabez and about serving God. He's a natural leader. He started a Jabez Club for kids. Its members have done free yard work for elderly people who could no longer care for their lawns. They've collected food and clothing for the county's homeless people. With every good deed, God got the glory. Everyone in town has said good things about Namid.

He's also a gifted ballplayer. This year when his team was playing for first place, Namid was on second base with his team down by one run in the final inning. Someone hit a soft single into left field, and Namid raced for the plate. It was one of those incredibly close calls, and the umpire called, "Out!"

As you've probably guessed, Namid is very passionate about everything he does. When he heard he was out, he lost his cool. He leaped up, argued loudly, kicked the dirt, and called the umpire a name. The people in the crowd couldn't believe their ears. This was the president of the Jabez Club?

By the next day, of course, Namid had cooled down. He knew his weak spot had been exposed. So, should he give up on his dreams? No, that would be much worse than what he had already done. He prayed, "Lord, I know You can do miracles, and my behavior yesterday set You up for a *big* one! Can You bring something good out of my failure?"

When he finished praying, he took out a piece of paper and wrote a letter of apology to the umpire. Then he wrote letters to the two teams. Finally, he wrote to the town's newspaper. He expressed his sorrow over losing his temper as he had. He also said that even though he was weak, Jesus is always very strong, and he wants his club to go on serving the town.

It was a miracle, all right. Some people were more impressed after his apology than they'd been before his failure. They could see that serving God isn't about never falling down. It's about having the determination to pick yourself up and move on.

Day Twenty-seven

TALK BACK

Today's reading has made me wonder about my weak spots. This might be one of them:

I want to prepare myself against messing up big-time because of my weak spot. Here is something I can do to be ready:

What if I do mess up, as Namid did? Here is how God might help me make the best of a tough situation:

WHAT'S THE BIG IDEA?

The race is won by the one
who gets up one more time than he falls down.

Day 28
The Light at the End of the Tunnel

You were full of darkness, but now you are full of light in the Lord.
So live like children who belong to the light.
Light brings every kind of goodness, right living, and truth.
Try to learn what pleases the Lord.

Ephesians 5:8–10 icb

Aisha had been through too much sadness. She felt as if she'd been moving through a dark tunnel for a long time.

She'd struggled through school. Aisha's dad just couldn't understand it. Aisha was obviously a bright girl. Why couldn't she apply herself a little more? Why couldn't she pay better attention in class?

Aisha had tried. She really had. But she always seemed on the verge of failing. There was even talk of holding her back a year. Finally, she took a series of tests with a special doctor. The doctor said Aisha definitely had something called attention deficit disorder—ADD. It meant that her brain was wired in a special way. Her mind was moving in so many creative directions that sometimes she needed a little help "tuning in" to her surroundings.

The doctor helped Aisha with her ADD, and her grades improved. I know you'd like to read that she lived "happily ever after," but it wasn't that easy. You see, Aisha had cried too many tears by that time. She'd told herself she was no good too often. It was like having a little cassette recorder in her head, always playing insults. The dark tunnel seemed to go on forever.

Hit the Switch!

Have you ever felt like Aisha? Have you ever felt that you weren't any good at all?

The truth is simple. God says you're the greatest! And remember, He makes all the rules. He has the only opinion that matters. And He loves you so much He gave His Son to die for you. He did it because He couldn't bear to spend the rest of eternity without you by His side. That's how deeply He adores you.

But it's hard to make that truth stick in your head, isn't it? If you make an A in school you might forget about it quickly. But if you make an F, it will likely stay in your mind, smoldering away. You have wonderful talents, but you focus instead on the things you *can't* do. Even though God says you're tops, all you can feel is that you're stuck to the bottom.

Today's verse reminds you that you live in the light, not in the darkness. God's Spirit has made a home within you, and He wouldn't move into a dump, would He? Our verse says He's busy building goodness, right living, and truth within you right now. So look in the mirror and see the kid God sees.

No, we won't get cocky—no chance of that, with all the mistakes you and I make. But we'll have a healthy understanding that God is an artist who paints with light. He makes beautiful, shining works of art—no cheap junk at all. In His workshop, there is no darkness. That stuff is the enemy's one and only product.

Into the Workshop

Aisha spent a lot of time thinking about her feelings. She kept coming back to the idea of walking through a dark tunnel with no light in sight. But as I told you, Aisha has a very creative mind. She asked herself, *Why not add my own ideas to this story?*

So she imagined a plot twist. In the new version of her word picture, she wanders down that dark tunnel, groping along the wall, and feels a door handle. When she pulls it open—*wow!*—the light floods over her, nearly blinding her. She stumbles into the room and discovers she's found the very workshop we've talked about—the one where the Father creates His beautiful masterpieces.

TRY TO LEARN WHAT PLEASES THE LORD.

She wanders through the room, fascinated. On the workbench, she sees a picture of herself. She catches her breath. It's the most beautiful picture she's ever seen. It shows an Aisha she could only dream of becoming: Aisha through the eyes of God. Beside the picture, she finds a book. It's filled with more pictures of her life, and every one of them shows the sides of things she never considered. All of it is beautiful. And the back of the book is packed with God's hopes and dreams for Aisha's life. But they glow so brightly she can't read them and know her future.

Aisha wishes she had sunglasses to handle the light and cover her tears. If only she'd known. If only she'd seen. At that moment, Aisha senses Someone standing behind her. She feels the gentle but powerful hand on her shoulder. And she knows she'll never walk in darkness again.

My friend, I hope you'll find that workshop, too. I hope you'll begin to see yourself as God sees you. After only a few moments, you'll realize there *is* a Light at the end of the tunnel, and you'll know exactly who shines it.

Already I sense you're picking up your pace, walking faster and faster to get there.

Into the WORKSHOP

Day Twenty-eight

TALK BACK

I've had times when I've felt down on myself. Here's the thing that usually makes me feel the worst:

_____

_____

_____

Today I've been able to see that the only opinion of me that matters is God's. Here's what I think He's saying to me right now:

_____

_____

_____

If I can hold on to that idea of how God thinks about me, my life might be a little different. Here's how I think it will change:

_____

WHAT'S THE BIG IDEA?

Inside every Christian there's a superhero trying to get out. Ask God to help you stop being a meek, mild bystander. Ask Him to help you discover your identity as a Christian crusader.

DAY 29
OVER-THE-TOP GOOD

*The Lord answered, "I will cause all my goodness to pass in front of you.
I will announce my name, the Lord, so you can hear it."*

EXODUS 33:19 ICB

IF WE HAD TO SUM UP all our time together in only three words, maybe we would choose these: *God is good.* That's why He blesses us. That's why we want to do more for Him. That's why He gives us power and protection. The question is: Just how good *is* God?

The answer is this: You'll never reach the far end of finding out. As you grow older, God will always give you more territory as you ask Him. Your dreams will grow, your blessings will grow, and your appreciation of His goodness will grow. There's never an end to God's goodness.

Jamal is discovering that now. He became a Christian a few years ago and began to pray every day. During the next few years, he learned more about God, trusting God a little more deeply. But during all that time, it seemed to Jamal that one thing was missing. He really wished he had a best friend. He thought it would be great to have someone his age to enjoy spending time with. Though he was becoming better friends with God, he also knew he needed a good human friend.

It occurred to Jamal one day that he had never told God these thoughts. He'd prayed to be a better Christian, a better son, a better brother. He had prayed for his class at school. But he'd never specifically asked God for a best friend. It seemed a little odd, but Jamal bowed his head, closed his eyes, and said, "God, could You send me a best friend?" In a minute, I'll tell you how it all worked out.

GOD IS A FRIEND, TOO

Don't ever forget that God is the best friend you have. You can go to Him as you would your parents, your pastor, or your favorite teacher at school. It's okay to tell Him exactly how you feel. Jamal had to learn that he could really open up with his desires to God.

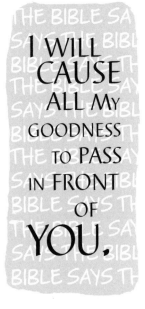

I WILL CAUSE ALL MY GOODNESS TO PASS IN FRONT OF YOU.

Have you ever been cleaned up, dressed up, and combed down for a big family reunion of aunts and uncles you'd never met? Once you were there, it probably felt awkward to be around so many unfamiliar relatives. They were family, but they were also strangers. That's the way it is when we first come to know God. At first, we're a little too stiff and formal with Him. We try hard to say the right things, and we don't feel comfortable enough to really be ourselves. But as we grow older and wiser in our relationship with God, we relax a great deal. Soon we can talk to God as if He were our very best friend in the world—as, of course, He should be.

As we said a few weeks ago, it's all right to ask God for your special needs. It's okay to ask Him for things that would bring you delight. He won't always say yes, of course. But God deeply desires you to open up your heart to Him. He wants you to know the very simple truth that *He is good.* And He wants the opportunity to show you His goodness through many blessings.

GOODNESS ON PARADE

Jamal's prayer for a best friend stayed on his mind during the next week. Just knowing he had made that prayer changed things. Jamal kept watch, halfway imagining a great big package would drop out of the clouds. It would be marked "Best Friend for Jamal." It was just a silly idea to make him smile, but he did feel God would answer his prayer.

Of course, God did. As Jamal looked across the cafeteria in school one day, he suddenly noticed a boy named Steve. He'd never known Steve very well, but he knew Steve was a nice person. He just hadn't ever felt the need to find out more about him. Now Jamal was conscious of having asked God for something, and he believed God's answer would come somewhere, sometime. He might as well go out and try to meet it.

So that day he took his lunch tray over and sat at Steve's table. The two of them talked about some things—football, music, television—and it seemed they had all the same likes and dislikes. It looked like the beginning of a promising friendship. Jamal felt certain this was God's answer, so he treated Steve as his best friend. He also made an effort to be the best friend he could be to Steve. I guarantee you that Jamal's faith grew about two notches. And so did his friendship with Steve.

God is *so* good. Remember to ask Him to show you this goodness—like Jamal did. A long time ago, Moses asked to see God's glory firsthand. The Lord passed by him and gave him a tiny glimpse of His goodness. It lit Moses up! Light shone from him as he left God's presence. As the goodness of God parades through your life, you, too, will light up this world.

Goodness
on
Parade
Day Twenty-nine

TALK BACK

I can think of several ways the goodness of God "lights me up." Here are a few:

I also know it's okay to ask God for things I really care about. I know there will be reasons why He has to say no sometimes. Here is something on my heart to pray about:

I want to know more of God's goodness all through my life. Who wouldn't? Below I'll list the things that I can do in my life to help myself experience more of His goodness:

WHAT'S THE BIG IDEA?

It's impossible to experience all of God's goodness, but it's a good idea to try anyway!

DAY 30
WHO, ME?

Then the Lord said to him, "Who made man's mouth?
And who makes him deaf or not able to speak?
Or who gives a man sight or makes him blind?
It is I, the Lord. Now go! I will help you speak.
I will tell you what to say."

EXODUS 4:11–12 ICB

"I THINK YOU'RE BIG ENOUGH NOW for a bike without training wheels." *Who, me?*

"I think you're old enough now to use the riding lawn mower." *Who, me?*

"I think you're mature enough now to go out and serve God." *Who, me?*

There are always times when you wonder, *Why not someone else? I'm not ready!* Moses felt like that. He was one of the Bible's greatest leaders, but it took a big shove to get him going.

Moses had been raised in a royal palace. But when he grew up, he had to hide out in the desert because he'd lost his temper and murdered an Egyptian. Moses hid for many years, probably thinking his life was ruined and over. Then one day he saw the bush. What a shrub! It burned, but it didn't burn out. That was odd enough. But when the bush began to talk, well, things had reached full-scale-crazy mode. A talking, burning bush! "I will send you to Pharaoh," said God through the bush, "that you may bring My people, the children of Israel, out of Egypt" (Exodus 3:10 NKJV).

This was definitely a Jabez moment. But Moses hadn't been out looking for one. The desert was enough territory for him, but not for God.

"Who am I?" Moses asked. (*Who, me?*) Then he went on to list all the reasons he felt unfit to be God's servant. He wasn't good with words. The Egyptians wouldn't believe him. Nobody there had heard of the Hebrew God. . . . Couldn't God send someone else?

And the Lord told him the same thing He tells us all: "Go! I'll be with you."

You're Elected!

When God calls us, He has His reasons. It's not about our abilities or our inabilities. It's not about our age or our readiness. It's all about the fantastic power of God. If God chose some incredibly talented hero for the job, there'd be less glory for the Lord. Instead, He always chooses to use people who aren't quite sure they're ready. Humble people, young people, and ordinary people. Do any of those people sound like you?

God let Moses run through his entire inventory of excuses, then He asked, "What's that in your hand?" (When the Lord asks a question, listen up. *Hint:* He already has all the answers!)

Moses looked at his fingers and replied something along the lines of, "It's just a staff. Standard equipment for a shepherd. Why do You ask?" And God showed Moses what He could do with a simple piece of wood. He changed it into a snake. He changed it back to plain wood. And soon He astonished a pharaoh.

Why did God ask that question? It didn't really matter what was in Moses' hand. It might have been a turnip and God still could have performed a miraculous feat with it. The more common and ordinary the object, the better. When it's used in God's service, God is glorified. And just as that rule applied to the piece of common wood in Moses' hand, it also applies to common people in God's hand. If He wants to use you, and if you agree to go, miracles can and will occur. Lives will be changed. Nations will be reborn.

So, what is that in your hand, and what can God do with it?

Raise Your Flag!

A few years ago, several teenagers from Burleson, Texas, were studying the Bible together over a weekend. They decided to pray together. They prayed with deep feeling, straight from the heart. They asked God to use them to make a difference. And wow! Did God ever answer their prayer!

During the kids' prayer time, God gave them new concern about their friends at three other schools. The kids finished praying, went out the door, and visited the three schools. It happened to be a Saturday night. The schools were locked up tight, so the teenagers stood around the flagpoles and prayed for the students of each school.

Somehow, their story spread all through the state of Texas. The idea of meeting at the flagpole for prayer got other kids excited. They wanted to pray for their schools, too. Before long, flagpole prayer meetings were happening all through the state. Then it became a *national* movement. Only a year after the first couple of students got together to talk to God, a million students had gotten involved in the movement called "See You at the Pole."

Miracles occurred in those circles as kids came to know Christ for the first time. And it all happened because several very ordinary teenagers asked God to use them. Could God be planning to shake the world through you?

Day Thirty

TALK BACK

Wow! I guess I can be ordinary and still be used by God. I think I know why God does it that way. It's because:

_____

_____

_____

I can see that all I need to do is be willing to let God use me. On a scale of one ("Me? No way!") to ten ("Here am I! Send me!"), here is how I would grade my willingness to serve God: _____ .

I'll also explain my grade here:

_____

_____

_____

I should ask God to use me every day if I'm willing for Him to do it. Here's a space for me to talk to Him about that:

_____

_____

WHAT'S THE BIG IDEA?

God loves to work through ordinary people.
I want to be one of them!

DAY 31
KEEP YOUR HEART ON TASK!

*Lord, you are the God of our ancestors. You are the God of Abraham,
Isaac and Jacob. Please help your people to want to serve you always.
And help them to want to obey you always.*

1 CHRONICLES 29:18 ICB

HE WAS ONLY A BOY, just one more child in a rowdy house filled
with them. But one day a stranger came and pointed at him, and
his life changed in an instant.

David was a young shepherd boy. He was most proud of having taken on a bear and a lion that had threatened his sheep. And
he had won! But then a man named Samuel came, looked him
over, and told everyone, "You're looking at the next king of Israel."
Imagine someone visiting your home and saying, "This kid will be
the president someday."

Without even knowing it, David stepped onto the fast track to success. Later, after he brought down a giant named Goliath, crowds
chanted his name. Soon he moved into the palace with King Saul.
Maybe was thinking, *Hey, I can handle this!* Then the bottom fell out.

Saul became jealous. David learned that Saul wanted to kill
him, and he had to run for his life. For years, he hid in forests and
caves, keeping one jump ahead of the king's armies that pursued
him. Can you imagine his thoughts? *Hey, Lord! What happened to
our agreement? You know, the one about the thrones and palaces?*

Once David had looked at kingdom-size borders. But then his territory was reduced until it was no bigger than the cave he slept in.

Many people never would have forgiven God for such a trial. "What has He done for me lately?" they might scowl and say. But David was made of tougher stuff. He kept his heart on task.

NEVER, NEVER FORGET

The rest is history. You can read the whole thing in your Bible. Things mostly worked out well for David, and he became Israel's greatest king ever. Then the time came when he was old and close to death. He stood before all the people of Israel and offered a prayer. You'll find part of it at the top of today's reading.

HELP THEM TO WANT TO OBEY YOU ALWAYS.

"Please help your people to want to serve you always," he prayed. Deep inside the gray-bearded old man giving that prayer lived a boy who had brought down a bear, then a lion, then a giant. The young man who had hidden in caves and fled from armies lived in him, too. David knew how important it was to hang on to his heart's desire for God.

So many things will happen as you grow up and move into the world. Some experiences may seem like the one at the Moby Coaster in the amusement park. Remember that one? You'll soar into the clouds one moment then plummet to earth the next. Hang on to your heart!

As old King David offered his prayer, a young man named Solomon stood nearby. Solomon, David's son, would become the next king of Israel. Solomon asked God to expand his borders in wisdom, and God did. He became a brilliant man who did great things. But he didn't hang on to his heart's desire for God. He didn't follow his father's advice. Solomon's life was so easy that he relaxed. He became lazy in his obedience to his Lord. And the entire kingdom suffered as a result. Don't let that happen to you!

THE GREAT WINDOW

Imagine you're walking down a tunnel. But this isn't any tunnel you've traveled before; there's no darkness here. This is a tunnel of pure light!

You walk past a sign that says, "Now Entering Heaven." You feel excited and curious. But you also feel a little nervous. God's favorites from throughout history will be there. You wonder about some of the things you've done in your life. Did you do enough for God? You almost wish heaven had a back door so you could slip in without attracting notice.

It turns out you've entered heaven during a big celebration. There's noise, laughter, and singing. Terrific! You can sign in quietly. But immediately someone grabs you by the shoulder. Then someone else, who introduces himself as Jabez! Soon you're swept high into the air and carried above the crowd. Are they angry at you? No, they're singing out your name! You must be dreaming. Everywhere you turn, there are tears of joy and happy shouts of welcome. This whole tremendous party is for *you*.

The others carry you toward a great window and throw open the curtain. The perfect, beautiful hills of eternity are filled with too many people to count. The scene stretches into infinity. A familiar hand rests on your shoulder and a voice says, "My child, these are the people you brought to heaven through your life's work. I enlarged your borders. And your response enlarged the borders of heaven itself."

This party is for you. All heaven is singing its thanks, but soon the singers turn their attention back to God, who deserves all the glory. You join in the singing as one more stranger walks up and hugs you. "My name is Jesus," He says. "I've been looking forward to shaking your hand."

Then you and all of God's partners live happily and *eternally* ever after.

Day Thirty-one

TALK BACK

What a time I've had with the prayer of Jabez! It's hard to believe I've come to the end. But it's really a beginning, isn't it? For me, the greatest single point I've learned through my Jabez journey is this:

_____

_____

_____

The biggest personal decision I've made about my life is this:

_____

_____

_____

I'm going to write my feelings toward God on a separate sheet of paper. First, I'm simply going to thank Him. Then I'm going to tell Him what I'd like to do for Him. These are ideas He has put into my heart through my Jabez journey.

Here's my signature and today's date:

_____

WHAT'S THE BIG IDEA?

God has planted wonderful seeds in your heart.
Water them and tend them, and you can spend
the rest of your life watching miracles spring
from the soil of your life.

Introducing more life-changing books from the author of the #1 *New York Times* bestseller, *The Prayer of Jabez*™

The Prayer of Jabez

Break through to the Blessed Life! Discover how God's miraculous power and experience the blessings He longs to give you.

ISBN 1-57673-733-0
The Prayer of Jabez Audio ISBN 1-57673-842-6
The Prayer of Jabez Audio CD ISBN 1-57673-907-4

Secrets of the Vine

Make maximum impact for God! Dr. Bruce Wilkinson demonstrates how Jesus is the Vine of life, discusses four levels of "fruit bearing" (doing the good work of God), and reveals three life-changing truths that will lead readers to new joy and effectiveness in His kingdom.

ISBN 1-57673-975-9
Secrets of the Vine Audio ISBN 1-57673-977-5
Secrets of the Vine Audio CD ISBN 1-57673-908-2

The Prayer of Jabez for Teens

Seeking the extraordinary for your life? Take the Jabez challenge of asking for blessing—and see how God answers extravagantly.

ISBN 1-57673-815-9
The Prayer of Jabez for Teens Audio CD
ISBN 1-57673-904-X

Multnomah Publishers®

www.prayerofjabez.com

"Like millions of other parents, when you first experienced God's limitless power in *The Prayer of Jabez*, I'm sure you wanted your children to share these blessings. Now you can show them how God desires to bless all His people—including kids. As we encourage the next generation of leaders to follow God's direction, we truly make the greatest impact on our future for Him."

—Bruce Wilkinson

The Prayer of Jabez™ for Kids
ISBN 0-8499-7944-7

The Prayer of Jabez™ for Young Hearts (picture book)
ISBN 0-8499-7932-3

The Prayer of Jabez™ for Little Ones (board book)
ISBN 0-8499-7943-9

SUPER-SIZE Your Faith

God is the One who really knows what makes us happy. He has great plans for you–blessings bigger and better than anything you've imagine if you will just trust Him.